# Turnip Pie

# Turnip Pie

### and other stories by

# Rebecca Cummings

Woodcuts by John Thompson

Puckerbrush Press, Orono, Maine

Cover design of mountain cranberries
by John Thompson

Two of the stories in *Turnip Pie*, "The Legacy" and
"Berrying," won the Chapbook Award of the Maine State
Commission on the Arts in 1984 and were published by
Coyote Love Press. "Berrying" also appeared in *The Best
Maine Stories: The Marvelous Mystery*, Lance Tapley,
publisher.

"Yellow Birch Tonic" appeared in *Inside Vacationland:
New Fiction from the Real Maine*, Dog Ear Press.

The story "Turnip Pie" appeared in *BitterSweet* as "The
Day George Pottle Had Turnip Pie." Also in *BitterSweet*
appeared "Another Miracle."

"The Wedding" appeared in *Kennebec: A Portfolio of
Maine Writers*.

ISBN 0-913006-36-X

*Printed in the United States of America
by Howland's Printing Company, Old Town, Maine
Bound by University of Maine Press*

In memory of the
grandmothers and grandfathers.


*Isoisien ja Isoäitien
muistolle.*




*With thanks
to
George Garrett
and
Madison Smartt Bell*

# CONTENTS

# TURNIP PIE

1907

Kaisa Kilponen's mouth watered in anticipation of the turnip pie she was making. Last Thursday, Hilja Kyllönen had given her three little blushing turnips, the first from her garden, and the thought of putting those sweet roots into a pie had been on her mind ever since. She was making enough so they'd have cold pie for Saturday supper, and since tomorrow was the Sabbath, enough for Sunday supper as well.

The sour rye-meal starter had been working overnight, and the bubbly sponge filled the wooden bowl. She mixed in handfuls of flour until she had a dough that was so stiff it wouldn't take any more and then kneaded it energetically, slamming it on the wobbly table top with a loud thump-thump. She cut off a big piece of raw dough, fit it into a pie tin, piled it high with slivers of boiled turnips, pork slices and lumps of fresh butter, and topped it with a crust. She rolled the remaining dough into fat round loaves, enough bread for the next week.

The bread her mother used to make back in the old country, in Finland, had a hole in the center so that the hard black loaves could be hung on a pole across the ceiling, but in

9

America they didn't do it that way. A lot of things were
different in America, but at least she and Matti, her husband
of nearly three years, had turnip pie and *sauna*.

Turnip pie. Nothing like it. Now if Matti would only get
home early enough, he could have some with her.

After breakfast that morning, Matti had rigged the horse
and wagon and had gone to Scab Mountain where he would
see about getting a pig. Not that going to Scab Mountain was
an all-day journey, but Kaisa knew very well that Matti
would probably stop by Erkki Suominen's, and then the two
of them would go down cellar together. So it could be some
time before she saw her husband again.

The large pie swelled in the oven and browned nicely.
And oh, what a heavenly smell! Just looking at it was enough
to make her hungry, but she didn't cut into it. She just left
it on the table to cool. But didn't it look good.

As soon as the bread had baked and was beside the pie
under a clean white cloth, she finished her inside work and
then took her scrub brush and heavy broom to the *sauna* in
order to give it a good scrubbing before lighting the fire.
As she scoured the floor and wash benches with coarse sand
and water, she thought more and more about the savory
turnip pie. The more she thought about it, sitting on the table
under the white cloth, the hungrier she got, and her stomach
gnawed in impatience.

Finally she set a match to the kindling under the rounded
mound of field stones. The fire would have to be fed all
afternoon so that by evening there'd be a bed of white coals
that would keep the *sauna* hot for hours. She then hurried
from the small smoke-filled building, thinking about turnip
pie. Just one piece. One little piece.

As she turned the corner to the house, she was surprised
to see a sprightly black horse harnessed to a shiny buggy.
Of course it belonged to George Pottle, their neighbor. He
was the only one for miles who had such a showy animal.
Sure enough. There was fat George Pottle standing in her
open doorway. Now why wasn't Matti at home? Like most
Finnish wives, Kaisa had never had any reason to learn
English since her husband did all the talking for the two of

them. But now here she was alone, and she'd be forced to
say something. Gripping the scrub brush and broom, she
approached him.

"There you are!" George Pottle bellowed at the small
woman, so slight of stature that she was barely to his shoulder.
"Where's Maddy?" He pronounced the name *Maddy* instead
of *Mut-ty*, the way it should have been said. "Where's
Maddy?" he again loudly demanded.

"No home! No home!" she said, shaking her head fiercely.

"No home?" George repeated. Then impatiently correct-
ing himself said, "You mean he's not at home?" Although
he was only a few feet from her, he continued to shout. He
always shouted at his immigrant neighbors. He seemed to
think that if he could only speak loudly enough, they'd understand. "That's a fine thing. Just fine." And he heaved a
huge sigh. The bother in having to deal with these people.
How did it happen that they had been able to get all these
little farms in Edom? Now they were all over the place, and
still more were coming every day. Each one of them sending
for sisters and cousins and uncles. There should be a law.
Perhaps he should write his congressman. Or go to Augusta.

"YOUR   COW!" he shouted in exasperation. "YOUR
COW IS IN MY CORN AGAIN!"

"*Cow?*" Kaisa repeated, not understanding at all what he
was making such a fuss about. Again she said the word.
"*Cow?*"

George Pottle stomped his foot, a surprisingly small foot
for a man of his great size, and let loose with a string of
profanities which it was just as well that Kaisa, a church-
going woman, did not understand. Again he sighed, much too
loudly. It then occurred to him that if he mimicked the motions
of milking, she might understand. Straining to keep from
toppling over, he stooped and pulled vigorously at airy teats.

Kaisa nodded her head excitedly. She understood!

George puffed back to his feet—it seemed that he was
finally getting somewhere—and jabbed his fat finger in the
direction of his corn field.

Suddenly, Kaisa clapped her hands to her face. The cow
was in George Pottle's corn! He had once warned that if it

happened again, he'd keep the cow. Heaving aside the scrub
brush but clinging to the broom, Kaisa whirled and started
off through the field at a run.

George Pottle, with an air of righteous self-satisfaction,
watched the small woman bob through the field, the white
apron strings flapping against her long dark dress. He
watched until he could no longer see the quaint maroon
kerchief that covered her hair.

That cow of theirs had caused no end of damage. This was
the third time it had strayed into his crops. Couldn't trust
those foreigners to tend their stock. And why wasn't the
man of the house home to take care of it?

Strange, these folks, dressing like that and washing up in
the queer way they did. He had seen the smoke pouring
from the little shingled outbuilding when he drove in. He
now knew that was where they took their baths. He remembered that the first time he had seen all the smoke, he had
thought their building was on fire. And then he had thought
that that was where they smoked meat. However, Albert
Hayes had told him all about it one night at grange.

It seemed that Albert had even gone into one of those
baths. He said it was like going into the jaws of hell, it was so
hot. That served Albert right, being so friendly to these
people and wanting to try everything.

It still angered George when he thought about the time he
had passed by one evening last summer and had seen the
husband and another man sitting outside that very bath house
without a stitch of clothes on. For all the world to see! It
was just as well that his Marjorie—bless her—was no longer
with him to have to see such sights.

And the things they ate!

Perhaps it was the smells of the freshly baked bread and
turnip pie wafting from the open doorway that made George
Pottle think of what they ate. But suddenly, George could
think of nothing but food. Not that the dark bread they ate
had ever appealed to him. That tough-looking bread could
never compare to the soft white bread his own mother had
taught his Marjorie, as a young bride, to make for him. For
a moment, it irked him that Marjorie had deprived him, by

passing on, of the bread he had grown used to for over forty years. Life was unfair!

However, the thought of the unfairness of life dissolved as the sweet image of Rose Parsons flitted through his mind. He wondered whether she could make bread. This latest housekeeper he had hired had turned out to be nothing but a disappointment.

He had to admit that the smells drifting from the kitchen were mightily appealing. He stepped inside to look and lifted the corner of the white cloth. His nostrils twitched. Four loaves, all rounded and plump. But what was that strange-looking puffy thing? Because he had had to dash over, he hadn't yet taken the time to have his dinner, and he was a man who liked to eat at twelve sharp. He bent over the pie and inhaled.

To be fair, George Pottle truly felt that these people owed him something. Wasn't this the third time their cow had gotten into his corn? All that damage! Not to think of the inconvenience. He puffed in indignation. So, at the moment, he felt quite justified in helping himself to the turnip pie. Just recompense, he thought. They owe me for my trouble. It's small enough payment.

As he held the reins of the prancing horse, he hungrily eyed the pie. His huge stomach rumbled. At last, with one hand, he tore out a small chunk from the pie so that pieces of slippery yellow turnip slithered through his fingers. Although he had fully expected that he would be throwing the whole mess to his dog Satan because it would be so foreign, he did nibble the bit in his fingers. Not bad. Not bad at all. In fact, it was tasty enough that he took a more generous bite. The turnips, pork and freshly churned butter had all made a gravy inside the hard crust so that the filling was rich and moist. And what flavor! He had never had anything like it. As the buggy jostled down the rough gravel road, he greedily ripped off more, the juices drizzling down his plump hand to be stopped by his shirt sleeve.

Now if George Pottle had known better, he would never have eaten in a single afternoon a turnip pie that had been intended for two generous meals for two generous appetites.

Never! Any Finn would have known better, especially if he had been planning, as George had, on finally asking Rose Parsons to become the second Mrs. George Pottle. Never! Anyone who has had turnip pie would have known better. But once started, George couldn't resist the pie, and he picked away at it all afternoon until it was gone.

As always on grange night, the street around the hall was lined with wagons and carts. Men, with their hair slicked back, milled outside in the warm evening air, smoking cigarettes and exchanging manly gossip. As George drove his buggy in, a small group disappeared around to the rear, most likely to share a covert flask.

Inside, the ladies, in their Saturday night finery, put out on the long cloth-covered tables, dishes of beans and pickles, cole slaw and hot biscuits.

George had no difficulty in finding Rose who, as always, was flanked by her two aging parents. George took a place across from the Parsons. Although he was not in the least bit hungry, to be sociable, he scooped a sizable helping of molasses-sweetened beans, a fair-sized portion of cole slaw and reached for two fluffy biscuits.

Adelaide Parsons commented on George's waning appetite and inquired whether he might not have a touch of the grippe that was affecting the area, but George denied any infirmity. "Just not much appetite," he claimed.

Adelaide looked knowingly at her husband.

Rose smiled up through distorting round eyeglasses. George Pottle might be nearly old enough to be her father and a bit more rotund than she had secretly dreamed her lover would be. But he was gentlemanly and would be a good provider. His was one of the largest farms around. She couldn't help but think of the future. There was no denying that her parents adored her, their only child, but time was marching on, and they wouldn't be able to care for her forever. She had thought of going to Lewiston or off to New Hampshire to work in one of the mills, but that thought frightened her.

When no one could take another bite, the ladies cleared away the empty serving bowls and platters, spent butter plates and pickle dishes, dirty silverware and water glasses.

At last, they folded their aprons and hung the dish towels to dry. The gentlemen, who had been biding their time outside, smoking and discussing the new model of thresher, pushed back the tables to make room for dancing. The Stowe Brothers Four Piece Orchestra, in shiny black suits and dazzling white collars, arrived and mounted the stage.

George hurried across the noisy hall to Rose who waited with her anxious parents. Just as he asked the pleasure of her company for the first dance, he felt a twinge of distress, a knot in his lower regions that twisted and turned.

George's pink face flushed scarlet. Sweat stood out on his brow so that he daubed at his head with his huge linen handkerchief. The sounds of the orchestra tuning, the talk, the laughter jangled against his ears. A wave surged through him, rising and falling, ebbing and flowing, like the tides at Old Orchard Beach. Rose, chattering about next week's picnic, clung to his arm as though she would never let go.

"One-and-a-two. . . ." Sammy Stowe directed from the piano bench.

The hall hushed.

The first notes of the Grand March resounded along with the gasses trapped in George's lower colon.

Rose gasped.

Harry Porter gibed, "Too many beans, George?"

Before Tom Record could say a thing, his wife Mavis jabbed her elbow so sharply into his side that he grunted.

Laughter broke loose.

The Grand March went on.

Rose fled for her wrap, insisting that her mama and papa take her home. George, however, bounded through the front doors out to the blessed relief of the cool night air.


As for Kaisa, when she finally returned home that afternoon wielding the broom behind the brown cow, she was as hungry as she'd ever been. After her cow was well tied, she went into the kitchen, prepared to cut into the turnip pie she had been thinking about all day. How surprised she was to find only the four loaves of bread under the white cloth.

Am I getting feeble minded? she wondered.   Did I only
imagine making it?   No, she knew she had made it, but it
was no longer there.   The door, she now remembered, had
been left wide open.   A peddler or a tramp?   Could a wandering peddler have come in and helped himself?   That had to
be the explanation!  What else could have happened?

Telling herself that the poor peddler must have needed
the pie more than she—Or why else would he have taken it?—
she appeased her hunger with a glass of cool buttermilk and
a thick slab of rye bread, spread generously with good churned
butter.

# ANOTHER MIRACLE

1908

When Kaisa Kilponen pushed down on the handle of the outdoor pump, cold clear water gushed into her bucket. The well had given pure, good-tasting water ever since they had lived on the farm. Until now, she had accepted the good water without question. But because of last Sunday's sermon, she couldn't take a cupful of water without examining it. She couldn't get that sermon off her mind.

She understood Jesus' healing the sick, and she accepted without question that Lazarus had come back from the dead. Those miracles were so great, of such magnitude, that she couldn't help but believe. What puzzled her, what gnawed at her mind, was Jesus' turning water to wine. Water to wine? How had he done it? So once again, as she had many times during the week, she studied a dipperful of her own crystal-clear well water, wondering whether or not it would happen that one day she would push down on the pump handle and bright red wine would spew forth. She'd have to talk to Matti about it when he got home.

Not that she'd ever had more wine than one has at a communion service. Her husband Matti, however, was another story. It was no secret that he liked his drink. Although some might have found reason to criticize, he was a hard worker and honest. A handsome man with fair hair, a lively golden mustache, and a ruddy coloring. His smooth tongue and easy manner earned him friends, even among the Yankees.

She now regretted that he had been able to talk her out of so much egg money for a trip to Canada to visit his cousin Eero. And if that wasn't enough, he had asked for a little more in order to bring back a bit of whiskey. Not for drinking, he had loudly assured her. But for medicine. Anyone could tell her, he had said, that whiskey from Canada made the best medicine.

Remember last winter, all the influenza? Kaisa remembered. It had been weeks before her chest cleared, and even now she had a trace of a cough. So with that argument, she had emptied the old woolen stocking of nickels and dimes and two silver dollars and had wrapped the coins in a clean white handkerchief. "For medicine only!" she had said.


When Matti returned home, he talked on and on about a Swedish tramp he had met in the railroad yards and about getting lost and finally he thought to show her the jug of clear amber liquid that he had brought home from Canada.

"But why isn't it full?" Kaisa asked.

"It's this way, wife. They knew that I'm from America, so they had to sell me a United States gallon, not a Canadian gallon. They had to take some out. Don't you see? It had to be according to the law."

"These laws. I will never understand them. But this one does seem particularly strange. Now tell me. How was it done? Did they just pour some out?"

"That they did!" Matti insisted, with a sharp slap on his knee. "I guess we should divide what's here and put it down cellar to keep it safe."

So with a nail, he etched the half-way mark on the side of the jug, and then he halved it again, so that the fourths were marked. "You can easily see, wife. Two quarters for you to keep as medicine and two quarters for me, since I did the buying."

Kaisa nodded. That seemed fair enough, although she still was not absolutely satisfied about the missing amount. "You say they just poured it out? On the floor or outside?"

"Not on the floor! Outside, of course."

Matti wasted no opportunity to slip into the cellar, and he had no end of excuses why he shouldn't. Haying was hard work. Hilling potatoes made him thirsty. The mosquitoes poisoned him. Why, a man needed to drink something after a hot *sauna*. So, of course, it was no time at all before he reached the first quarter mark and was proceeding towards the half-way point.

When the contents of the bottle met the second mark, Kaisa reminded him that whatever was left belonged to her to keep as medicine. They had made an agreement, and she would see that he lived up to it.

He said that he knew full well what the agreement was and would not think of touching her share.

She said that she was only reminding him.

He said that he preferred coffee anyway. And to prove his point, he stirred another gritty spoonful of sugar into his milky coffee and drank it down in one gulp.

Matti still made trips to the cellar, but now he carried his hammer and nails and maneuvered long boards with a good deal of cursing and muttering through the kitchen and down the steep stairs. He had to make new bins, he said, for the fall potatoes and turnips. And then he had to see to the foundation under the kitchen. She knew it was rotting, didn't she?

One day after he had come up from the cellar and had gone back outside, Kaisa, clinging to the railing, descended the wobbly stairs into the dark dirt cellar. She pulled the bottle out from between two chinks of cobwebbed rocks and took it upstairs into the light. The brownish-red liquid sparkled at the point where the sunlight streaming through the kitchen window glinted on the second etched line. What kind of wife am I, she asked herself, to be so full of doubts about the trustworthiness of my husband?

And because of her little guilt, she prepared a tasty fish pie, just the way Matti liked it with a thick crust, from the yellow perch Wäinö Mustonen had given them the evening before. Kaisa was satisfied, and then with all the work of summer, she eventually forgot about the jug in the cellar.

What made her remember the whiskey was a letter from her friend Aino Leino who said she would be coming from Rockland to spend a week with Kaisa in October. It had been several years since Kaisa had seen Aino. As young girls, they had traveled the steamship together to America, but after they had married, they had gone separate ways, each with her husband. Time had a way of passing now between visits.

Although Kaisa had never approved of a woman's partaking of spirits, she knew that upon occasion Aino took some drink. So as she made preparations for her visitor, Kaisa thought about the jug in the cellar. Maybe she should offer a little of her share to her friend. Aino would be, after all, a special guest.


What pleasure the two friends had, eating all the good food Kaisa had prepared and going over old times. They talked and laughed so hard that, more than once, they had to wipe the tears away.

On the last evening of Aino's visit, Matti threw up his hands, saying that the two women sounded like two crows on the roof, that he was going to bed. Kaisa saw her opportunity and scooted down to the cellar, coming back with the whiskey from Canada.

"A little of this will help make your visit here a pleasant memory," Kaisa said, holding the jug high for Aino to see.

"Only if you will have some too. To keep me company."

Kaisa hesitated. She had never intended to try some with Aino. But after Aino continued to insist, Kaisa at last assented. "Only a bit," she said, a reckless tingle coursing her spine as she poured the amber liquid into two water tumblers. "Matti says it's the best you can get. It's from Canada."

"I've heard that in Canada they make the best. *Kippis!*" Aino said, raising her glass in toast.

Kaisa watched expectantly as Aino drank. Aino's small eyes rounded in surprise. She held the glass up to the lantern to examine it. "Humph!" she said, sniffing at the glass and drinking again.

Kaisa sipped warily, unsure whether this first drink would send her sprawling to the floor. She swallowed. It didn't taste at all as she had expected. She hadn't known that whiskey would taste so much like— Now what did it taste like?

"Does this whiskey taste like— ?" Aino asked.

"Coffee!" Kaisa cried. "It tastes like coffee. Is that how they make it in Canada? More?" she offered.

They sat at the kitchen table in the glow of the lantern light, telling again the stories they had told all week, laughing and crying and laughing some more. They emptied their glasses and filled them again.

"I should go to bed," Aino at last said with a huge yawn. "So much traveling tomorrow."

"And I'm tired too." Kaisa gripped the edge of the table to help herself up. She, too, yawned, although she didn't feel in the least sleepy. But she was anxious to get to the loft bedroom. There was something she wanted to ask Matti.

Once in bed, Kaisa nudged her husband who was already asleep, but he merely turned over and began a wet, noisy snore. Bracing herself on one elbow, she kicked him so hard in the legs that he woke with a start. "What? What?" he blubbered in sleepy confusion.

"The whiskey! It tastes like coffee. Why does it taste so odd?"

"The whiskey?" her husband said in groggy bewilderment. "The whiskey? Ahhh— !" he nodded, at last awake. "Were you at the whiskey?"

"Aino— " Kaisa said quickly. "You know how Aino— "

"But of course it tastes like coffee! Anyone knows whiskey that is kept too long turns to coffee. It's your own fault for trying to keep it for so many months. Now why did you wake me? You know I'm a working man!" With that, he turned his back to his wife and resumed his snore.

"It does?" she said, puzzled.

Kaisa lay with her eyes open long into the night. The fact was, she had not known that whiskey would turn into coffee. And, of course, before this she had never tried drink. She had never wanted it. But now that she had been tempted—

She stared at the vague dark shape that was Matti's back. And then, she understood.

Of course! It was another miracle! The good Lord who looked over them all had transformed it into coffee. He had done it to keep her from developing a taste for whiskey. It was that simple.

She reached over and lovingly touched her husband on the shoulder. With the mystery resolved, her eyelids drooped, and she at last slept.

# COUSIN KENU

1909

Kaisa Kilponen peered from behind the shadow of the kitchen curtain as Alfred Stout reached from the wagon seat and lifted the lid of the mail box by the road. After his horse plodded past, Kaisa tied her everyday maroon kerchief over her hair, threw a tattered shawl around her shoulders and practically ran to the box, she went so fast.

Even though she could read in Finnish as well as the next one, having learned on her mother's knee back in Finland, and she saw that it was her name in the spidery blue scrawl, she placed the thin white envelope on the high clock shelf between the two front windows. Later, they'd read the letter together, she and her husband Matti.

Several times that morning, Kaisa interrupted her chores—scrubbing the kitchen floor, baking bread and turnip pie, mending Matti's work pants—to go to the clock shelf, reach for the envelope, and turn it over, only to put it back beside the ticking clock. It was not a letter from Finland but from Massachusetts. Who could be writing from Massachusetts when everyone she knew in America lived right there in Edom or in the nearby county seat?

Shortly after the clock chimed eleven, she began to listen for Matti, although she knew it would probably be close to twelve before he came in. The table was set. The bread was sliced. A savory stew bubbled on the back of the stove. At last she heard the scraping and clumping of feet at the door as he cleaned his boots. Leaving the kitchen door ajar, she hurried out into the woodshed.

"There's a letter!" she blurted.

"A letter?" Matti said, leaning a crowbar in the corner. "I guess it's not the first one we've had."

"Yes, but this is for me. From Massachusetts." Kaisa kneaded her hands in the folds of the clean apron she had put on in case the news was bad. "Why would I be getting a letter from there?"

Matti was clearly in no hurry. He sat on the chopping block and slowly unlaced his muddy boots. "We'll soon see, won't we?" he said.

But rather than take the letter from the shelf, he unbuttoned his shirt and hung it on a hook by the door. Then he dipped hot water from the reservoir on the side of the stove into a small wash basin. Shoving back the sleeves of his undershirt, he washed himself at the kitchen sink.

At last, his shirt back on, he reached for the letter, examined the handwriting and said, "Let's see who is writing to you." He unfolded his pocket knife and slid the blade beneath the flap. Kaisa bit her lower lip. Although she stood with her back to the heat of the stove, she shivered.

"It's from your cousin Kenu. He, too, is in this country and has been in Massachusetts for three years staying with some relatives of his father's. Now he's coming to Edom to visit. He says that he saw your mother and sisters in Finland before he came and will bring you greetings from them. He should arrive within the week." Matti refolded the letter and placed it back in the envelope before handing it to his wife who took it with a shaking hand.

"Kenu is coming here?" Kaisa exclaimed as she read. "And he's seen Mother and my sisters?" She smiled, fighting to keep her eyes dry. "I'll have to clean if we're to have company. He'll be here within the week. And baking! There's baking to do. Why, I was only a girl— '' In her mind she again saw the thin, tow-headed boy who so often had been the brunt of older boys' pranks.


It was a cool moonlit Saturday night, long after *sauna* and supper. In the circle of lamp light at the kitchen table, Kaisa pedaled the butter churn, worked five knitting needles around the heel of a sock, and read aloud from the second book of Corinthians. With the soft slapping of the churn and the droning of his wife's voice, Matti's head drooped and he dozed. It had been a hard day, and he was tired. Since the cemetery was but a short distance away, Matti was the church-appointed caretaker and digger of graves. That day he had dug a grave for old Kosti Heikkinen who had answered his Maker's call the morning before.

Just as she was about to turn the page, Kaisa heard a faint knock at the door. She looked up, dropping the needles.

In his sleep, Matti snorted.

Again, Kaisa heard the knock.

Kaisa shook her husband by the shoulder. "Matti! Matti!" she whispered.

She stood behind her husband as he opened the door. It was a stranger who stood there, nervously clutching a round hat.

"Do you know—? That is to say— '' the stranger stammered. "Is this the home of Kaisa Kilponen?''


Her face flushed, Kaisa bustled about the kitchen, warming a rice pie and making coffee. Her own cousin, she thought. Right there inside her kitchen. She scooped out an extra spoonful of coffee. For a relative, she wouldn't be niggardly.

To Matti, this cousin of Kaisa's didn't look like much. Too thin. Hardly bigger than Kaisa herself. And nervous. As he sat, Kenu's feet twitched and he pulled at his ear. Not knowing what to say to this cousin whose pale eyes darted from one thing to another about the room, Matti asked, "How was your trip?''

"Trip? Trip?" Cousin Kenu stuttered, twisting his ear so that it had turned bright red. "Not good. Not at all." He wiped his hand across his brow. "My traveling bag, you see, was stolen. Everything I had is lost. The thief ran off so quick. I tried to stop him, but— That is to say, I couldn't remember the words in English. I started for the police and saw that I would miss the train, so I had to turn back."

For an awkward moment, Matti thought that Kenu might cry.

"And I got off at the wrong station. That's why I've arrived at such a late hour. South Edom, not Edom. How was I to know they were different stops? I tried to ask the conductor, but he told me to move along." Kenu blinked back his distress and slid his fingers into his vest pocket for a small ivory-colored comb which he flicked through his thin colorless hair.

Matti glanced at Kaisa, slicing meat at the work table, and then at Kenu. Kenu was more womanish than she.

"A farmer saw me and offered to— That is to say, a farmer gave me a lift in his wagon. I had to walk from the village, though."

Matti had never seen one of his countrymen who was so dainty. Most were plain hard workers.

"The worst— " Kenu lowered his voice, whispering, "was the cemetery. I went past Satan's handiwork. An *open* grave! Thank the good Lord, I found your house."

"Oh, that— " said Matti, thinking to tell Kenu about Kosti Heikkinen.

"I should have expected it!" Kenu continued. "Bad luck comes in threes. I lost my traveling bag. I got off at the wrong station. And then— " Once again, he ran the little comb through his hair and patted it into place.

"That's foolish!" Matti scoffed, wondering whether or not this Kenu was a drinker and, if so, whether he might possibly have a little something left over.

"It's the truth!" Kenu shrilled, waving his comb at Matti. "Think about it. It's based on the Trinity!"

"Why— " Kaisa said thoughtfully, a sharp knife in her hand. "Why, yes. The Father. The Son— "

"And the HOLY GHOST! that's right. That's it."

"I think you'd better eat," Matti said, barely hiding a sneer. He turned to his wife. "Hurry, woman. Get your cousin something to eat."

Kaisa took the rice pie from the oven and set it on the table along with a dish of fresh butter and a plate of cold sliced beef. She poured two cups of steaming coffee, one for Cousin Kenu and the other for Matti.

"Rice pie!" Kenu exclaimed, wetting his lips with his tongue. Suddenly, his hands were everywhere, pouring a huge dollop of cream into his coffee, scooping up a heaping spoonful of sugar, spearing a slice of beef, and reaching for the generously large pie.

With many starts and stammers, Kenu told and retold the events of his arrival to the stream of visitors who came to greet Kaisa's newly arrived cousin. Each time he told his story, the string of events became more significant. And each time he told his story, he settled more comfortably into being a guest.

Because he was a guest, Matti, for the first week at least, hurried through his chores so that he would be free to walk Kenu around the newly cleared fields or into town to buy a starched collar or scented soap for shaving. And because Kenu was a guest, Kaisa prepared hearty meals and set coffee tables with plates of the cardamom-flavored sweet bread she made so well, fat cookies and doughnuts, all be-fitting one who had seen her mother and sisters in Finland, albeit three years ago.

Kaisa soon saw that what Kenu said about bad luck coming in threes was true. If she broke an egg while hurrying to gather them, she was sure to spill the cream as she skimmed it from the top of the can and then bang her shin on the edge of the grain bin. Or if she nicked her finger with a kitchen knife, she'd drop a piece of firewood on her toe and forget to switch the bread baking in the oven from top to bottom so that it burned. Now that she was aware of it, it seemed that bad luck did, indeed, come in threes.

The summer was a busy one. Because the spring had been cool and cloudy, the hay was slow to ripen. And when it was at last ready to cut, there was rain, day after day. Finally in the middle of July, the weather cleared, and then Kaisa worked feverishly alongside Matti to bring the hay in. With the rains, wild mustard, pigweed and witchgrass grew so fast among the potatoes and turnips and corn that it was all Kaisa could do to keep them at bay. In her spare time, she picked quarts of wild berries—strawberries, raspberries, blueberries and blackberries—which she stewed with sugar in huge batches over the heat of the woodstove and put up in steaming glass jars. If the day were slack, Matti would back a load of firewood to the woodshed door, and together they stacked it in neat even piles, row upon row, ready for winter.

The cows and hens and pigs needed to be watered and fed

twice a day. There were clothes to be boiled and scrubbed. The house to be kept clean. Meals to be prepared. Coffee for the visitors. And day by day, the corn ripened.

All the while, Kenu made himself comfortable, wandering off after one meal and appearing just before the next.

Matti might have tolerated Kenu's lack of ambition had Kenu been made of sterner stuff. But because Kenu would quake if he met his own shadow on a sunny summer afternoon, he earned Matti's wholehearted contempt. A crashing thunderstorm would send him into spasms of fear. The thought of walking the road after dark kept him in the kitchen each evening. And the feisty gold-and-green tailed rooster strutting through the dooryard was enough to turn Kenu, at a run, back for the kitchen where he would grope for the little ivory-colored comb as though it were the talisman that protected him from devils of all sorts.

Unknown to Kaisa, Matti encouraged a lively hatred in the big rooster towards his guest by plaguing it with Kenu's stiff brown hat, until all it took to work up a furious rage in the bird was for it to see the hat approaching. With a noisy squawking and a dusty flapping of wings, the rooster would attack and force Kenu's retreat. For Matti, who more often than not had tossed the fowl into Kenu's path, there was no funnier joke. Many a time, he could have been found around the corner of the barn or woodshed, wiping away streaming tears of laughter with his handkerchief.

One Sunday evening while Matti and Kaisa attended services at the newly built Lutheran Church at the corner, Kenu remained behind, nursing a touch of indigestion. Dusk had just settled into darkness when Matti and Kaisa returned. They found Kenu, white with fear in the kitchen, babbling about spirits upstairs. When Matti, shrugging off his wife's grip, found that a squirrel had crawled in through the eaves and had chewed a hole in the corner of the featherbed, Kenu tried to laugh off his fright. Each time he cleared his throat to begin another stammering explanation, Matti sniggered. Finally, Kaisa quieted her husband with a sharp remark.

Early one morning in mid-September, Kaisa draped freshly washed bedding over the clothesline. Hearing the racket of geese overhead, she looked up, shading her eyes to watch. Yes, it was to the south they flew. There had even been a touch of frost that morning.

And just that morning, Matti had trailed Kaisa over the frosty grass into the cowbarn. As she sat beside the brown cow, her cheek to its heady flank, the warm milk spurting into the bucket, Matti had said, "Kenu must go! He mooched from his father's relatives for three years. Now he thinks he can do the same here."

"But we can't just ask him to leave— " Kaisa didn't look at Matti but concentrated on her milking. The yellow barn cat, its tail high, scampered to Kaisa, rubbing against her leg. "He is, after all, my relative." The cat mewed, rubbing back and forth.

"He may be your relative, but he's worthless. He doesn't want to do a thing around here. All he does is comb his hair when he gets nervous about something. That's why he's losing it. He combs it so much. Look at mine," Matti insisted, smoothing back his own blond hair which, in reality, was getting thin as well. "I don't comb mine but once a day, and look at how much I have. And that soap he uses! It smells funny. To say nothing about how he eats. Did you see last night? He ate over half the turnip pie!"

"Perhaps I should have made a larger one," she offered lamely. But Kaisa had noticed how much Kenu had eaten last night and the night before. He was her relative, though, the only link she had to her mother and sisters back in the old country.

She remembered a time, some two or three years after she had been married, when she had been overwhelmed with homesickness. Matti had been away for the day, and she was alone in the house. All morning she had thought about her mother and sisters, Anni and Liisa, wishing she could see them, talk with them, give them coffee here in her own house. For a while, she made herself believe it were possible. She covered the table with her best cloth, set coffee cups for three, put a plump glazed braid of *nisu* on a board. She sat for coffee, smiling, seeing her mother as she had last seen her, Anni and Liisa on either side. They talked and laughed about so many things—about when they were young, the other relatives, the price of goods in America. At last, though, aching with loneliness, she picked up the coffee dishes and wrapped the braid of *nisu* and put it back on the pantry shelf. She had never spoken to Matti about that day, had never mentioned it. Now he wanted to ask Kenu, the only relative she had seen in years, to leave.

"Just a while longer," she pleaded. "Let's wait and see what his intentions are." She got up from the low stool, pushing the yellow cat aside with her foot, and poured out a cup's worth of warm milk into the tin plate. Then she remembered, "Why, just yesterday he helped me in the kitchen! He cleared the dishes from the table."

"Woman's work!" Matti snapped. "One more week. One more week, and then I'll ask him to leave." With that, he strode out of the broad cowbarn door.

But during the week, something happened to divert their attention. Erkki Seilonen, late in getting his second crop of hay and hurrying in the face of a fast approaching storm, suffered a terrible tragedy. A sudden clap of thunder startled the horses, and his mother, on top of the haywagon with a pitchfork, fell and broke her neck. At such a time, it no longer seemed fitting that Matti should ask his guest to leave.

The next afternoon at the cemetery, Matti met Wäinö Mustonen who sometimes helped to dig graves. Like Matti, Wäinö had his tools, a pickax and spade. Although Matti had clear, cold well water in his jug, anyone could see that it wasn't well water that Wäinö carried.

"To keep us cool, my dear friend, if the afternoon grows warm," Wäinö said, "or to keep off the chill should it grow cool."

Matti smiled, for Wäinö always spoke as though his tongue were coated with honey. Surely, he thought, the work will go easier.

Actually, there was nothing at all easy about the work. They broke through the heavy clay, only to hit rocky ledge. As the afternoon wore on, they shed their shirts. Taking turns, one dug while the other shoveled. Each time they changed positions, they passed Wäinö's jug.

Finally, late in the day, they both descended into the deep pit to admire their work.

"Nice— " Matti muttered, lodging his spade into the damp gray clay. "Very nice— She'll— Rest in peace." He mounted the handle of the spade in order to leap out but wobbled and fell. He tried again, and taking the spade with him, vaulted clumsily into the warm sunshine.

Matti stumbled to his feet. "Wäi-nö— " he called.

Wäinö didn't respond.

Matti rooted his heels into the sod and reached down into the grave. "Take my hand, Wäinö."

But Wäinö didn't take Matti's hand. Instead he blinked twice and fell. Sprawling in the grave, Wäinö slept, the empty jug nestled against his chest.

Matti picked up his tools and, juggling them from one arm to the other, started for home.


Perhaps worried that he might be called upon to assist in digging the grave, Cousin Kenu that morning had borrowed enough egg money from Kaisa so that he could take the train to the county seat shortly after breakfast. The agricultural fair was to open the next day, and he thought to get a first-hand view. He whiled away his time, strolling about the grounds as the concessions took form. He ambled back and forth through the exhibition hall, greeting the ladies of the grange as they arranged sparkling jars of pickles and preserves and tacked brightly colored hooked rugs and delicate crocheted doilies to the walls. He struck up a lengthy but pleasant conversation with plump Glenna Matson who was assisting her mother in piling a pyramid of orange pumpkins near the entrance to the baked goods booth. After some polite conversation, Glenna's mother allowed her daughter to accompany Kenu through the dusty grounds, past the tent that hid the freaks of nature and the burgeoning carousel.

If Kenu hadn't found Glenna's smile so winsome and her endless prattle so charming, he surely would have started

back for Edom much earlier.  But as it was, the sun hung
heavy and red in the western sky when he finally bid farewell.
With a last good-bye, he promised to look for her near the
pumpkins the next afternoon.

Fortunately—for Kenu had already missed the train by an
hour—a passing buggy offered to take him to the general
store in Edom.  As the nag lumbered off, leaving him alone in
the growing darkness, Kenu's heart sank.  He started down
Edom's Main Street and, too soon, left the friendly lights of
town behind him.

For Kenu, the dark shadows hid unknown terrors.  Each
night sound evoked unspeakable fears.  He walked more
quickly, the gravel crunching underfoot.  Hearing a rustling
in the dried ferns and grasses, he giggled nervously and
groped for the familiar rounded teeth of the little pocket
comb.  Kenu hastened on, breaking into a run when a falling
acorn bounced on his shoulder.

The closer he got to the Kilponen farm, the closer he got to
the cemetery.  And the closer he got to the cemetery, the more
clearly he could envision the gaping wound, the hole waiting
to be filled, the very grave Matti had been digging just that
day.  Even though the night air was cool, Kenu's shirt clung
wetly to his back.

In the dim starlight, he made out the vague shape of the
stone wall that ringed the little cemetery.  Kenu's fingers
flicked through the sign of the cross as skillfully as a Bishop's
at an ordination service.  Beneath his coat, his heart thumped.

Strangely enough, though he wanted to hurry past, to
embrace the comfort of Kaisa's tidy kitchen, to wallow in
the warmth of the featherbed, an inexplicable curiosity
had gripped him, was pulling him through the gate, past
the thin stones to the dark mound of earth.

Soft clods of fragrant soil crushed beneath his shoes.  Then
he stumbled, his toe hitting a round pebble.  The small
pebble bounced in the air and rolled into the open pit.

Wäinö, who had been asleep in his cool damp chamber
for some hours now, was awakened by the hollow plop of the
pebble.  Thinking that Matti was there, he groped stiffly to
his feet and trilled in a clear sweet voice, "Is that you, my
charming friend?"

Kenu never looked back.  He pitched over the shadowy stone wall and clambered across a stubbly hay field, not stopping until he reached the dooryard of the little farm.  Unmindful that Kaisa and Matti were already in bed and asleep, he dashed up the stairs to his side of the loft and stuffed his few belongings into one of Kaisa's embroidered pillow cases. For the remainder of the night, he kept vigil at the kitchen table, the lamp turned so high that the chimney blackened with soot.

The next morning, just as the rooster crowed, Cousin Kenu left for town.


Kaisa was surprised when she began her breakfast preparations that she hadn't heard Kenu stirring.   Thinking he must still be asleep after his late night—for she had heard him come in—she called to him from the bottom of the stairs. When he didn't answer her second call, she timidly climbed the steps and peeked around the edge of the flowered curtain to his side of the loft.  Except for the pillow, now stripped of its case and tossed carelessly to the floor, the bed was untouched.  All that lingered of Cousin Kenu was the faint perfume of scented soap.

"Isn't it strange that Kenu left so fast?" Kaisa said to her husband as she buttered a thick slice of rye bread at breakfast.   "He didn't even say good-bye.   And what do you suppose he was doing out so late?"

"Hmmm— " Matti said, thinking that perhaps Kenu had known which way the wind was blowing after all.

The group of mourners was gathered at the grave site. With head bowed, Pastori Halme delivered the lengthy final prayer.    Matti, through half-closed eyes, caught the glimmer of a white object nestled in the weeds and loose dirt at his feet.    With his toe, he nudged it, recognizing it immediately, for in the past months he had seen it many times. But what was it doing here?  He frowned in thought.

As the prayer ended, Matti fought back a smile tugging at the corners of his mouth.  He shifted his weight to cover with his foot a small ivory-colored comb.    Along with the others, he said, "Amen."

# MR. MURDOCK,
## A SALESMAN OF FINE WATCHES

1909

That winter, Matti left his wife Kaisa tending the farm in Edom and went to the lumber camp in order to earn enough to meet the taxes and, perhaps, even to buy a woodlot of his own.

The camp was like many another that dotted the Maine woods. There was a bunkhouse furnished with what was basic—a water barrel, a tall stove, and a hay-covered bed, wide enough to sleep ten to a dozen men, running the length of one wall. Behind the bunkhouse was a two-roomed cookhouse where Leena Hakola, the frowzy-haired cook, both slept and worked. And because there were Finns in the camp, it was no time at all before there was a *sauna*.

One Saturday in February, Leena made room at the already crowded supper table for a stranger who had appeared earlier that afternoon, having come in on the provisions sledge among the sacks of flour and sugar, cans of kerosene and crates of beef. His name was Mr. Murdock, and he was a salesman of fine watches.

The lumberjacks, in a confusion of languages—English and French and Finnish—dug into the fare set on the rough plank table, beans with chunks of salt pork, flat biscuits and

sweet pickles. Matti, sitting beneath one of the two lanterns
that shone overhead, ate with his knife, skillfully balancing
runny beans and pickles. Although Matti had never had baked
beans before coming to America, he had quickly taken to
them and ate them now with hearty appetite. After three
helpings of beans, salty though they were, four or five biscuits, slightly burned, and a side of sweet pickles, he sighed
and sat back, his thumbs hooked under his leather suspenders.

Mr. Murdock, wearing a shiny vest and white shirt, frayed
at the cuffs, sat across from Matti. The salesman was a
small man, thin and slight of build, seemingly even smaller
amongst the muscled woodsmen. He ate delicately, his
little finger high.

Leena, nervously bird-like, picked her way behind the
noisy table, leaning over the men to pour mugs of powerful
black coffee. With her free hand, she shoved the crockery
bowl in front of Mr. Murdock. "Eat. You eat-a ta beans,"
she insisted, a wad of tobacco bulging in her cheek.

The beans Leena served were salty and the biscuits burned.
But Mr. Murdock, thinking of the small line of ladies' watches
he carried, scooped out another heaping spoonful of beans
and slapped them on his plate.

"You make good beans," he said, speaking loudly enough
that everyone looked his way. "Delicious."

Leena grinned, her blackened teeth showing, and poured
coffee for the heavily bearded Canadian next to Matti.

Mr. Murdock swallowed, his Adam's apple bouncing.
"And what a biscuit," he continued, now that he had the
attention of the table. "Crisp." He bit into it, dribbling
flakes of biscuit onto his vest. Then to Matti opposite him,
who hadn't spoken at all during the meal, Mr. Murdock asked,
"Do you—? Speak English?" He knew that these fair-haired
Swedes, or whatever they were, were ripe for sales. Once
they started earning good American money, they couldn't
wait to spend it. There wasn't a one of them but didn't
covet a pocket watch of his own.

"Speak-a ta English?" Matti thumped himself on the
chest. "I speak-a ta good English."

"May I interest you—after dining, of course—in my line of fine watches? I feature Waltham, a name of excellence."

The fact was, Matti had never heard of Waltham, nor any other brand of watch. But each time a man reached into his pocket to check his timepiece, Matti thought how he would like to be able to do the same. Yes, a watch was just what he wanted. However, since coming to America, he had learned about shrewdness, so he bit into a piece of pale flat cake and said, "Nah! I no need no vatch."

"A fine line," Mr. Murdock persisted. And to Jaakko beside him, "For you? A new watch?"

"I got ta good vatch," Jaakko said, reaching into his pocket and pulling out his nickel-plated watch. "See. Last year I buy ta vatch." Then Jaakko asked off-handedly, "You like steam bath?"

Matti caught Jaakko's eye and quickly gazed up at the hand-hewn rafters on the ceiling as though nothing interested him more than how they were joined to the ridge pole. He added, "You take *sauna. Then* ve talk about vatch."

Jabbing his sharp elbow into Mr. Murdock, Jaakko said, "You take *sauna* vit me and Matti and Sulo." He jerked his big thumb at a short darkly-mustached man with powerful arms at the end of the table. "Sulo be part Russian, but he be good man. Maybe he need ta vatch."

Mr. Murdock reached for the worn leather valise at his feet. He had heard about such baths. But if that was what it took to sell to these foreigners, he'd do it. He'd been selling long enough to know that the one across from him was more than ready to dip into his earnings. "Just what I need," he said. "A hot bath. Then I'll show you my line."

Mr. Murdock tipped his round hat to Leena as he left the cookhouse behind the woodsmen, and said, "Tasty meal, Ma'am. Very tasty."


In the dressing room, Mr. Murdock undid each tiny button of his shiny vest, shook out the wrinkles from his frayed shirt, unlaced his black boots—pulling the strings until they were just so.

He knew that the three Finns, already undressed and gibbering in their strange language, watched his every move with uncommon interest. He was now wishing that he hadn't agreed to this bath. He had, after all, bathed earlier this same month.

The door clattered shut against his haunches, so that he jumped skittishly into the dark washroom. Foggy shadows of the naked men stretched and leaped along the sooty walls and onto the low ceiling like a tropical shadow play of secrecy and evil. The swell of heat was enough to suck the very breath from his lungs. He stumbled, falling onto a low stool, feeling relief at being close to the cool floor.

The prick of light from a kerosene lantern, shining through a single small pane of glass inside the dressing room, glinted on a white shoulder, a forearm, a thigh. The chattering woodsmen turned bundles of dried cedar switches over the searing rocks of a hive-shaped stove and drizzled cold water over the brushy ends. Sweet steam sizzled forth. What design had they for these switches? Mr. Murdock had heard about strange things. There was a hotel in Bangor—

"When we're through," Mr. Murdock wheezed, wobbling to his feet, thinking to divert them, "I'll show you—"

Sulo, ignoring him, hoisted a bucket of cold water to a perch that ran beneath the low ceiling and climbed onto it. Jaakko followed.

"You go," Matti laughed, twitching the wet switches against Mr. Murdock so that he bounded nervously up the steps.

The heat on the perch was scorching. Mr. Murdock, wedged between Jaakko and Matti, panted. Every fiber, every tendon pulsed. His temples throbbed, and his skin prickled.

Suddenly, Matti, using a long-handled dipper, poured cold water from the bucket over his own head. Spluttering, he switched the cedar branches against his shoulders and then flailed Mr. Murdock's shoulders as well.

Mr. Murdock squirmed.

"You too hot?" Matti asked, looking past Mr. Murdock.

Mr. Murdock nodded.

"Here." Jaakko offered the dipper to Mr. Murdock. "Trow it on da rocks."

"Cold vater make you be cool," Sulo added, nodding his head as he spoke.

Mr. Murdock looked from Sulo to Jaakko and then to Matti on his other side. Pinpoints of light danced in their eyes.

He filled the dipper and with a mighty heave, threw icy water against the fiery rocks.

There was an explosion so sharp that Mr. Murdock thought the rocks had shattered. A cloud of hot steam gushed, enveloping the perch. Mr. Murdock moaned, hiding his face between his knees.

They roared. Hooting, Matti slapped his thigh. Jaakko clutched his sides, tears streaming down his cheeks. Sulo whooped, throwing out more water that cracked and sizzled as it hit the stove. The steam, dense and heavy, misted his eyes. Mr. Murdock felt a flicker of flying switches over his heaving shoulders.

He struggled to get down to the floor. Never in his life had he been as wretched. Grabbing his ankle, Jaakko held him back. Sulo threw still more water. Hot steam hung thick around them. The springy switches slashed the air. A withered swatch of cedar landed on Mr. Murdock's knee, glued in his sweat.

"Oh, my God!" Mr. Murdock gasped. "Oh, my God!"

At last , Matti wiped the back of his hand over his face and climbed down.

"Think about sales—" Mr. Murdock muttered, following him. "Think about sales—"

On the cool floor, they washed from wooden buckets. Then the three whisked the salesman, whose legs had no more substance than pale apple jelly, out the doors into the cold black night.

Mr. Murdock, flapping his arms and sighing, lay back in a snowbank, his eyes closed to the starry sky above.


Since it was Sunday, Matti had time after breakfast the next morning to stroll beside the salesman down the tote road.  A dusting of new snow had fallen in the night, and the sun now glistened on a clean new world.

At last, offering his hand, Matti said good-bye and watched as Mr. Murdock, who seemed to have found new bounce and vigor, headed out of camp.

When the salesman rounded the turn, Matti hurried back to the warmth of the cookhouse where Leena cleared the remains of breakfast from the long table.

"Come in!  Come in!" she greeted, speaking their own language.  She bent for the jug at the end of the table and spit into it a mess of yellow-brown tobacco.  Wiping her hands across her greasy apron, she went to the huge black stove in the cooking area to pour two mugs of coffee and then slid onto the bench opposite Matti.  She leaned over the table for the sugar bowl, and as she did, her work dress pulled taut to reveal the glint of a bright black ribbon around her thin neck.

"He sold you a watch, eh?" she asked, stirring sugar into her coffee.  "I knew he would.  That's why he went to *sauna*."

"A man needs a watch," Matti responded lamely.  He pulled the solid-feeling timepiece from his pocket.  "Silver," he boasted, holding it at such an angle that it caught the gleam of sunlight from the window.

"And Sulo?  Did he buy a watch?"

"A good one."

Leena examined the black Roman numerals, turned the watch over, cradled it in her hand.  "How much?  Seven dollars?  Eight?"

Matti shrugged.  He felt a flush of shame, remembering the taxes, the woodlot, his wife.

She handed the watch back to him.  "When he went to *sauna*, I knew he'd sell you one," she laughed.  She blew over the rim of the steaming mug.

"What's that you have on?" Matti asked, noticing the edge of bright black ribbon over the top of her round neckline.  "Something new?"

Leena's hand leapt to her throat.  "Nothing."

"You bought a watch!"

Her fingers fluttered.  "But I need to know the time.  Need

to know when to cook a meal. When to go to sleep. I need to know just as much as anyone." From the front of her dress she pulled a dainty gold watch dangling on a piece of new black ribbon. "Pretty, eh?" she asked.

"That Mr. Murdock, he liked the beans, did he?" Matti razzed, slipping his own new watch back into his pocket.

Leena stroked the face of her watch with her thumb.

Matti gulped his coffee and got up to go. Stretching, he said, speaking in English, "You make-a ta good beans, Leena." His blue eyes twinkled. "Dee-licious."

# YELLOW BIRCH TONIC

1910

It seemed to happen almost overnight. One day Matti had a full head of yellow-blond hair which he slicked back with water whenever he washed, and the next, his hair came out by the handful so that his scalp showed, shiny and bald. Matti was quick to blame Cousin Kenu's comb, which he had pocketed after the funeral for Erkki Seilonen's mother. He threw it away, but still his hair grew thinner.

More than once that winter, Kaisa walked into the kitchen to find her husband arranging what little hair he had so that it covered the receding hairline. The first time, Matti jumped aside and busied himself with brushing the dust from his shoulders. The second time, he complained about a bruise on his forehead, although Kaisa couldn't see a thing there. The third time, he opened his mouth to examine his molars.

"You fool!" she snapped. "Of course you're going bald. You're getting on in years, aren't you?"

The remark stung. He wasn't yet thirty.

Matti felt a pang of envy each time he saw a healthy head of hair. Sitting behind the Nurmi brothers in church, he saw that they had no less hair than they had ever had. And Sulo

was three years older than Matti.  Amos Cole, the proprietor
of the Edom General Store, had a plenteous mass of wavy
hair, snow white though it was.  And as Matti sat in Barker's
Barber Shop with a hot towel over his face, he watched as a
mound of curly hair piled up under John Thompson, the
blacksmith.

It was towards the end of mud season, but still well before
spring planting, when Matti hitched the horse to the express
wagon so that he and Kaisa could go for a visit to Erkki Seilonen's.  Kaisa, wanting to take some little gift, carried on her
lap a glass jar of maple syrup, freshly made only three weeks
earlier.  After Matti and Kaisa had learned to tap the sugar
maples that grew along their eastern boundary, they boiled
the clear sap into dark sweet syrup each spring to spoon over
breakfast porridge, hot biscuits and puffy oven-baked pan-
cake.

"This syrup reminds me," Erkki said, eyeing the sparkling
jar on the table, as his wife Mari and their robust daughter
Este scurried to prepare the meal while talking with Kaisa,
"that sap from a birch tree is supposed to cure baldness."

Although he pretended that it didn't matter to him, Matti's
ears were open wide.  After a little silence, he asked, "Fresh
or boiled?"  But then he said, as though more weighty matters
occupied him, "If you don't have enough seed potatoes this
year, I've got some to sell."

"Fresh.  Not boiled," Erkki said.  "Rubbed onto the head
before meals.  Three times a day."  Erkki reached into his
pocket for a worn leather pouch and tapped stringy tobacco
into a scrap of newspaper and then, licking it along the edge
to seal it, added, "I've got more seed potatoes than I need.
But you might want to see Viljo Heikkinen.  I think his rotted
in the cellar."

"We'll stop by on our way home.  Uh—The sap of a birch?
It runs late, doesn't it?"

"After the tree buds."  The end of Erkki's cigarette flared
as he lit it.  "Yes.  After the tree buds."  He exhaled white
smoke from his mouth and nostrils.

"Hmmm— " Matti said.

It was a morning bursting with promise of the season to come. The air fresh. The sky clear and blue. After having given the matter considerable thought, Matti chose his trees, two healthy yellow birch. Yellow birch rather than white or gray, yellow being the color that most nearly matched his hair.

Crossing the lower field which was wet and spongy from the steady rains of the days before, Matti carried a drill and two buckets, one clinking with the two spouts inside rolling back and forth. Muddy water gushed under his boots.

Clear sap spurted as soon as he pulled the drill bit from the hole. In excitement, Matti wet his hands under the steady run and rubbed the cool sap over his head. He was immediately disappointed that other than the sticky wetness, he didn't feel a thing out of the ordinary. But of course it's too early, he told himself. This will take time. After all, a baby doesn't grow hair overnight. He set his buckets and hurried off, swatting at a swarm of pesky black flies.

It was nearly noon when Matti returned with two empty jugs and was amazed to see that the buckets were almost full. He poured the sap into jugs and hung the buckets back under the spouts. Again he wet his hands with the clear sap and slathered it onto his head. And again he fought off a cloud of biting black flies as he hurried home through the wet field.

The black flies chewed his arms and neck and head when he made his third trip, late that afternoon. Although the buckets were spilling over, Matti could see that the run was nearly spent. But with four full jugs, he had enough to grow more hair than he'd be able to handle. Unless he were willing to sit in Barker's barber chair once a week, his hair would probably be longer than any of the prophets. He could almost swear that this time he felt a little tingle to his scalp. Wouldn't Kaisa be surprised to see him with a full head of hair! *Old man*, she had started calling him. Why, he'd be looking five years younger before she knew it. Maybe even ten!

That evening while Kaisa was busy in the back room,

Matti examined his milky scalp in the oak-framed mirror. Could it be that he saw a yellow-blond wisp or two more?

*Sauna* was a dilemma. He wasn't sure whether or not to wash his head. He certainly didn't want to tamper with the beneficial aspects of the yellow birch tonic, but he had always been particular about cleanliness. Even in his lumber camp days, when some of the men didn't wash for a whole season, Matti had been the one to insist on building a *sauna* and heating it at least once a week. So sitting on the low stool in *sauna*, he started to pour a bucket of water over his head but then stopped. Once he had hair, he decided, he'd wash it all he wanted. There would probably be so much that washing it would be a nuisance. But for now, he would scrub only to the hairline, leaving his scalp free to grow hair. Anxiously, he touched his fingertips to the top of his head, sticky from the steam and sweat.

For the next few weeks, Matti trekked to the cellar before each meal to rub a generous handful of yellow birch tonic onto his scaly scalp. Kaisa's lips tightened with each anoint- ment. In the evenings she thumbed through the leather- bound Bible, seeking those verses that would speak to her husband.

"Ah-ha, old man!" she cried out, laying her knitting needles aside and running her finger along the lines as she read aloud from the book of Samuel. "I would say this is proof enough. It's perfectly clear that if Absalom hadn't been so vain as to let his hair grow long, he never would have gotten caught up in that oak tree while out riding. And then be fair game for his enemies, hanging by his hair. Here it is. The word of God. Right in the Holy Bible. Now throw that stuff away!"

"Throw it away? It's God's will that I ever learned to use it!"

"God's will?" She waved an empty knitting needle in his face. "Remember the Psalm? 'Who shall ascend unto the hill of the Lord. . . ? He that hath clean hands . . . who hath not lifted up his soul unto vanity.' "

"But don't *you* remember that 'All is vanity . . .'?" Then he added, with a triumphant smirk, " 'And VEXATION of the spirit'!"

In the last week of June, summer settled in with a fierce vengeance. Each morning, for days on end, the sun rose through a reddish glow, the air thick and heavy. Each afternoon, Kaisa watched as huge white thunder clouds mounted over the hills to the west. She waited for the crack that would break the spell, but the clouds drifted off. At night, Matti and Kaisa tossed on limp, damp sheets in the airless loft. Even though Kaisa had pulled back the flowered curtain that covered the doorway to the spare room and had opened the windows at each end, not a breeze stirred.

It was early one afternoon when Matti hung up his scythe and said that he was going into town. It was too hot to work. And besides, the hay chaff had stuffed his head. Then he sneezed, a wet, spattering sneeze.

Kaisa finished the ironing and swept the woodshed. She got the cows and did the evening chores. Since Matti still hadn't returned, she ate supper alone and then went to bed.

Late though it was, Kaisa lay awake and heard the squeak of wagon wheels. She could tell from the way Matti stumbled as he climbed the stairs to the loft that he had stopped by Väinö Mustonen's to cool off on the way home. As soon as Matti touched the pillow, he began to snore. Kaisa slipped out of bed and tiptoed down the stairs to go outside and sit on the front stoop.

A whippoorwill shrilled its unbreaking call from beneath a shadowy apple tree on the far stone wall. Again and again. Does it ever stop? she wondered. Doesn't it stop to breathe? The night air was damp, and the grass was wonderfully dewy under her bare feet. She closed her eyes, leaning her head against the rough wood of the door frame.

In her tiredness, she thought about the child, a son, delivered in its fifth month last winter. She relived the sorrow. Were they never to be blessed with children? A farm without children?

She almost dozed. And then from across the field, its faint cry started again. *Whip-poor-will. Whip-poor-will.*

The sun the next morning was hot and red. At breakfast,
Kaisa was already sticky from the heat. When Matti complained that the bread was stale, she snapped, "Maybe you'd
better learn to bake your own bread! I'd say it's good enough
for someone who doesn't know to come home at night."

She sat at the table and spooned her gummy rice porridge
listlessly. There was a fetid smell in the kitchen, and she got
up to sniff the drain in the black slate sink. But the problem
didn't seem to be there. The motionless air in the close room
and the rank odor were so overpowering that she took her bowl
outside and sat on the still shaded front stoop.

While Matti drove the brown horse in front of the hay
rake, Kaisa pulled the cumbersome bull rake along the edges
of the field. Hay was too valuable to lose even a trace. She
paused in the shade of a spreading apple tree. It wasn't even
mid-morning, and already it felt like mid-afternoon. She
shoved her wet, stringy hair, falling out of its bun, away
from her face. She had never known such heat. It had never
been so hot back in Finland.

She watched through weary eyes as Matti, on the far side
of the shimmering field, kept an eye on the mounding windrow
behind him as the horse made the turn towards where she
stood. Matti twisted in a sneeze. And then again. She
waited for another. There. He pulled his handkerchief from
his pocket, flicking it like a banner, and swiped it over his
face. The horse, its head low, continued plodding towards
her, over the buzzing field of freshly cut hay, spotted with
fading daisy and dying purple vetch. She could smell the
heat of the horse as it drew closer.

"I forgot to tell you," Matti called down from his perch on
the iron seat of the hay rake, "that I saw Pastori Halme in
town yesterday. I told him to come and eat with us today."
He took off his hat and rubbed his arm over his glistening
head.

"What? To do what?" For a second, Kaisa thought that
Matti had said that Pastori Halme was coming to eat. The
heat seemed to be affecting her.

"There's no need to make a fuss," he said climbing down from the rake. "Just what we always have." He went for the water jug, nestled amongst the weeds at the base of the tree. His shirt stuck wetly to his back. He pushed at his straw hat with his thumb and tipped the jug to drink. Water ran down his chin and neck. Catching the dribbling water to the back of his hand, he said, "And he's bringing the visiting pastor." He held the jug out for Kaisa.

"What? What are you talking about, old man? What visiting pastor?" Kaisa eyed her red-faced husband in annoyance. His nose was peeling, and the birch sap was slimy along the edge of his hat. She ran her dry tongue over her lips, but she didn't reach for the jug.

"Pastori Salminen! Have you forgotten? From the synod. He's come for the annual meeting and the picnic on Sunday. I told them to come here for dinner today."

"PASTORI SALMINEN?"

"I told you. I saw them in town— "

But Kaisa had already dropped the bullrake and had started for the house.

Now what? Her mind raced as she slid over the slippery hay. A visiting pastor? For dinner? What could she possibly do so late in the morning? She had been planning on fried pork rind and potatoes. But for a visiting pastor? She held her skirt high, so that her black stockings showed to her knees, and leaped over the rows of raked hay. She couldn't give fried pork rind to a visiting pastor. But what else was there? She turned the corner of the barnyard, past the little hen-house. A hen? But there wasn't time.

The screen door to the kitchen clattered behind her as she hurried through with an armload of wood to feed the dying embers. In the rising heat, she peeled potatoes and threw them into a kettle to boil and then thought to also boil a half dozen eggs. Scurrying to the garden, she grabbed for a huge handful of tender beet greens.

As the pots bubbled on the stove, she carried a pitcher of tepid water up the stairs to the stuffy bedroom beneath the eaves. She tore off her work clothes and, clad only in her modest undergarments, splashed water from the porcelain bowl onto her face and along her forearms. She quickly dried with the linen towel that hung over the harp and went to the mirror to pull her light brown hair back into a tidy bun, pinning it tightly with two wide-toothed combs. She slipped into her long-sleeved dark blue Sunday dress and arranged the white crocheted collar. With a final pat to her hair, she scooted down the stairs.

In the kitchen, she whisked her best lace cloth onto the wobbly table. She pulled one of the straight-backed chairs into the pantry so that she could stand on it to reach her company dishes, egg-shell colored with tiny roses around the rims, all stacked on the top shelf of the cupboard.

She anticipated the thick, heady odor of cream and the still, cool darkness of the milkhouse as she turned the handle of the door. Standing in the shaft of light, she blinked away the dimness. How pleasant to sit on a sawdust-covered chunk of ice and idle away the afternoon. The thought flirted with her imagination for only an instant. Instead, she reached for a star-stamped block of sweet butter and dipped fresh, cold milk from a wide-mouthed can into a glass pitcher.

She sliced the hard-boiled eggs into a milky gravy and spooned it over crisp pieces of pork rind. She cut thick slabs of rye bread and dished out the steaming potatoes and beet greens.

As she carried a deep, cut glass bowl of ruby red strawberries swimming in sweet juice to the table, Matti flew past her through the kitchen and down the cellar steps. And as she put down the dessert saucers, he raced back to go upstairs and come down again in his brown wool suit. The screen door banged behind him as he hurried out to sit in the speckled shade of the towering maple tree in front of the house with Pastori Halme and the visiting Pastori Salminen. Kaisa's nose twitched. That odor again. Where was it coming from? She heard Matti sneeze. Once. Twice. And then the murmur of voices.

Everything was ready. The table set. The food on. She went to the window, standing just behind the gauzy curtain. Even in this heat, the visiting pastor's suit was stiff and prim, the white collar tight. She had been so busy she had forgotten

how hot it was. She daubed at her face and neck with the hem
of her long apron. And tired. She had never felt so tired.
She thought about the cool, dark milkhouse with its smell of
cream. How wonderful to go in and not come out at all.


". . . and for this food set before us, we thank Thee, O
Lord," Pastori Salminen prayed, his voice as reedy as he was.

"Amen," they said, the men sitting at the table, Kaisa
standing by the stove.

The two men of the church and Matti helped themselves
to the meal Kaisa had so hastily prepared. Pastori Halme and
Matti heaped their plates with potatoes and greens, smother-
ing them with pork rind and gravy. Pastori Salminen, however, took only a spoonful of this and a bit of that.

A sluggish breeze wafted through the kitchen. That smell
again! What was it? Kaisa sidled to the sink and sniffed.
It was no more the drain than it had been earlier. She looked
around.

"Have more?" Matti offered.

"Thank you, but no."

Silverware chinked against the plates.

A fly buzzed over Matti's crusted head. He shooed it away,
his arm stiff in the tight suit.

"How long will you stay in Edom?" Matti's voice was thick
and nasal. He snuffled.

"Until Monday. Then Portland. I have relatives— "
Pastori Salminen eyed the buzzing fly.

Kaisa watched him watching the fly. Again she caught the
smell.

"The haying?" Pastori Halme asked. He was shabby
and faded beside Pastori Salminen. Something should be
done. Some sewing. She'd talk to the women.

Once more, Matti mentioned the heat.

The walls pressed inward. Kaisa tugged with one finger
at the scratchy crocheted collar. How could those men of the
clergy wear such tight collars?

The fly perched on Matti's shoulder. If she could only
grab for a newspaper from the corner cupboard. But not

with company. Not with Pastori Salminen. Matti shrugged it off while shoveling another dripping knifeful of potato and gravy.

Pastori Salminen picked at the greens with a fork. "Your head? A disease?" he asked.

"Ah, it's— " Matti faltered. He was half-standing, stretching across the table, reaching for more of the gravied pork rind.

But Kaisa was there before her husband could touch the serving dish, shoving it at the visiting pastor.

It was then that she knew.

And so did Pastori Salminen, for she saw in horror that he took a starched white handkerchief from his breast pocket and held the folded cloth to his mouth and nose.

It was Matti! Her own husband. The yellow birch sap had gone rancid. And with his hay fever, he hadn't smelled a thing. The fool!

She grasped the serving dish, refusing to give it up to him. Spots of heat enflamed her cheeks. "Have more!" she demanded of the visiting pastor.

Pastori Salminen dropped his handkerchief, looked to her flustered face and dipped out a scant spoonful of pork rind and gravy.

"More!"

Pastori Salminen drizzled a stream of gravy along the lace tablecloth.

"What's that?" Pastori Halme grunted, scraping his plate clean with a thick crust of rye bread.

Matti had loosened his shirt collar even before Pastori Halme's little black buggy had left the dooryard. He lost no time in getting upstairs to change back into his work clothes and stretching out in the thin grass under the maple tree to let his meal digest.

Kaisa, listening to her husband's snores, at last sat down to eat. What a dunderhead Matti was, she thought. As though birch sap could grow hair. As though he needed hair to be a man. When she finished her meal, she resolved, she would take the matter into her own hands.

Leaving her dirty dishes on the table, she slipped down the stairs into the dank cellar. One and a quarter jugs of the putrid sap left. Lugging the slippery jugs back up into the bright kitchen, she poured the cloudy liquid down the drain, following it with a bucket of hot water and lye.

She was standing on a chair, putting the last rose-rimmed plate back on the top shelf of the pantry cupboard when Matti, his eyes heavy and the side of his face red and creased with the imprint of grass and leaves, came into the kitchen.

"There's no need for you to go down cellar for more of that sap," she said, not looking at him as she got down from the chair. She closed her nose to the rancid smell.

"Why not? What are you talking about?"

"Couldn't you tell? It spoiled. It smelled worse than pig swill. I threw it out. Down the drain." She shoved the chair back to the table.

"Can't a man have a thing in his own house?" Although Matti blustered, he had been beset lately with doubts about the efficacy of yellow birch tonic. But he felt it necessary to add, "It's working. I can feel it."

"All you feel are the flies biting your head!" However, her voice sweetened and she said, "A man as young as you doesn't need to worry that losing a few hairs will make him an old grandfather. Why look at all you do. Enough for two men. Two *young* men."

Matti shrugged, annoyed, but he said, "Two?"

"We don't have a hired hand, do we? A hot day like this— Why don't you go out to the pump and wash your head? Think how refreshing it will feel."

"Well— " he said, scratching his head, smearing the sweaty sap. "Only because it's such a hot day." He started out but paused, holding the screen door open. "That Absalom must have looked pretty strange with so much hair. What do you think?"

Kaisa folded her large white dish towel, embroidered along one edge with purple violets and tiny green vine, and hung it over the rack to dry. Cocking her head, she listened for the noisy squeak of the pump outside.

As though blown by the push of the pump handle, the
curtains ruffled, and a sweet breeze floated through the room
like a soft whisper. Kaisa sniffed. Rain. She went to the
window.

Mountainous gray-bottomed clouds swelled in a murky
sky over the western hills. The undersides of the leaves of
the maple tree flashed silver as they whipped skyward.

"Matti!" she called, rushing outside. "Look!"

But Matti, his thin wet hair slicked back, was already
harnessing the horse to the hay wagon. Hearing a far-off
rumble of thunder, Kaisa grabbed for a pitchfork and hurried
to meet him, out in the hayfield.

# THE LEGACY

1912

The clock between the two front windows struck three times and then ticked on. In the dark, Kaisa Kilponen groped for a match from the shelf above the slate sink and struck it against the top of the cook stove to light the lamp. Her head was thick from lack of sleep, but her mind churned with all there was to think about. She sighed, a quick little sigh, and turned to make a small fire in the stove, just enough to take off the nighttime chill. After putting the tall enamel coffee pot on to boil, she went into the shadowy sitting room to fumble in Matti's oak desk for writing paper, pen and ink.

When the coffee was finally ready, Kaisa sat at the table, her new round table, lifting the edge of the heavy flowered oilcloth to run her finger along the shiny veneered top. For months she had saved soap labels and, at last, the table was hers. How she had had to struggle to hold back her excitement the day Matti brought it home on the express from the train station. But now, as she smoothed down the strong-smelling cloth, her past pleasure was thin beside the forebodings of the day ahead.

Kaisa gulped from the cup of steaming coffee and started

the letter to her mother in Finland. She told about the table, the fine harvest, the good health with which they were blessed, bits of gossip of this person and that. She hesitated, the pen poised. That other matter. Should she mention it?

She breathed deeply and continued, the pen scratching against the thin paper. *Today*, she wrote, *Matti becomes an American citizen. For him the wait has seemed long. It was a full year ago that he filed his papers, and today he goes before the judge.*

She stared at the dark window. No, she would say nothing more. Abruptly, she finished, *God bless you, mother. Kaisa Kilponen.*

She folded the two thin sheets of paper and thrust them into an envelope.


Unlike his wife, Matti had had a fine night's sleep. For him, the day ahead was ripe with expectation. As the morning sun crept through the windows of the kitchen, he shaved at the black slate sink. And he spent more minutes than even on a Sunday morning in front of the beveled bedroom mirror, slicking down his thinning hair and waxing the ends of his golden mustache.

Barely tasting the warmed-over beans and rye bread, Matti left the table when his breakfast was but half-eaten. He checked the time of his heavy silver pocket watch against that of the ticking clock. There was plenty of time. The train from Edom wouldn't leave until 7:30. He glanced at Kaisa, sitting stolidly at the table, her face set as she ate the dripping beans. For Matti, the years of waiting were over. The nights of study and memorization of citizenship lessons and lines from the *Declaration of Independence* were past.

"I can vote now," he said. "At this year's elections, I can vote for Teo-dorr Rrroo-se-velte!"

"If we were in Finland, *I* could vote."

"What do women know about voting?" he scoffed, as though that were the real issue between them.

Kaisa listened as the big brown horse plodded out of the dooryard, straining to hear as the express wagon clattered along the dirt road. Inside her was a ball of anger so hot that it was ready to explode, faster than a Fourth of July firecracker. Feeling as she did, there was but one thing for her to do.

Work.

Rolling the sleeves of the shapeless tan housedress above her rough elbows, she tackled the mound of wash belonging to their neighbor George Pottle. Last spring he had come by in his new-fangled automobile. With the engine chugging, he had remained perched on the high leather seat, shouting until Kaisa had timidly gone outside. By some means or other, for Kaisa didn't speak English and George Pottle surely didn't speak Finnish, he led her to understand that he was offering her as much as one dollar a week to do washing for him and the new Mrs. Pottle. One dollar! How could she refuse? So now, he brought the dirty wash by every Monday evening.

Wielding a thick wooden paddle, she stirred the clothes in the boiler on the back of the roaring stove and then hauled still another bucketful of steaming water from the hot water reservoir to the tubs on the washbench in the back shed. She rubbed the fresh bar of yellow soap over the striped shirt and scrubbed it along the coarse board.

Ever since she had come to this country, Kaisa had yearned to return to Finland. She had always thought to go back with money in her purse for her family. Her allegiance was to her people in her homeland. Of late, though, there lurked, in the deepest recesses of her heart, the inkling that she might not go back. That now she was tied to this new country.

She had to admit that life was more comfortable than what she had ever known. There was the little house and barn. Nearly forty-five acres. Three nice milking cows. A pig fattening for November slaughter. And she was earning good American money, with the eggs and taking in washing. It wasn't that she was not grateful. She said her Thanks daily. What was really eating away at her was the question of their *name*.

Mr. Mason, the lawyer who represented many of the
Finns in their quests for citizenship, had recommended that
Matti take advantage of his day in court to change his name.
At no additional cost, Mr. Mason would prepare the papers
so that at the very moment Matti Kilponen became an American citizen, he would also become MATT KILTON, a name
Mr. Mason had suggested. A name not so far removed from
Matti Kilponen, a name Mr. Mason could but barely pro-
nounce. The new name would assure Matti's easy assimila-
tion into the culture of this magnificent free country. On any
voting list, Mr. Mason had claimed, as he flicked the long
ash from his reeking cigar to the oiled floor of his dowdy
office, no one would ever be the wiser that he was anything but
American-born.

Having been fired with zeal for Theodore Roosevelt and
the Progressive Bull Moose Party, Matti looked forward to
exercising his right to vote. To Matti, no figure better ex-
emplified the ideal of American accomplishment than did
Teddy Roosevelt. Roosevelt's colorful exploits excited Matti's
imagination and earned his wholehearted admiration. To
Matti's way of thinking, Roosevelt was the very person who
had opened the doors of America to him. And now that he
was again running for president, Matti was anxious to give
him his vote. So Mr. Mason's mention of the voting list was
all the persuasion Matti needed. He readily agreed that the
name should be changed.

"KEEL-TUN!" Kaisa had gasped. "KEEL-TUN! What
kind of name is that? When I married you, I relinquished my
own good name, Hannula, and took your name, Kilponen.
And now you say it is not good enough for this country!
What about your father? And grandfather? Have you forgotten their legacy to you so quickly?"

Matti winced. Fleetingly, he had thought about his father,
dead now for ten years. And his grandfather whom he but
barely remembered. It *had* seemed as though he might be
forsaking them themselves and not just a name. That thought
had needled him until, at last, he had managed to shove it
to the back of his mind where it rested uneasily. Until now.
Until Kaisa once again brought it to the forefront.

"Many have done it!" he blustered. "Erkki Hiltonen shortened to Hilt, didn't he? Has he suffered? And what about Toivo Pulkkinen? Doesn't he go by the name Pike? Look at what a smart man he is. Already making so much money."

"Making loans at high rates to his fellow Finns!"

"Americans can't even say our names. Life will go easier with a Yankee name."

"Don't be a fool. You'll deceive no one about your origin. As soon as you open your mouth, anyone can tell you are not of this country."

"Pfff!"

"I— I— " she had stammered, her face growing hot. "I will NOT have that name! If you change the name to KEEL-TUN, I will use my own name again. Hannula was the name I was born with, and that will be the name I will die with!" Her head had throbbed, unused as she was to speaking so heatedly to her husband.

But change their good Finnish name?

Never!

Kaisa threw the undergarment she had just scrubbed into a tub of blueing.

It was then that she heard the crackle of a footstep outside. There was Hilja Kyllönen, walking heavily, wrapped in a thick black coat and kerchief, despite the warm September day. As a rule, Kaisa would have been happy to see the older woman. Hilja was not only a purveyor of news of every Finn in Edom, but she somehow knew the comings and goings of many of the Yankees as well. However, today Kaisa scowled as Hilja tottered towards the shed door.

"Kai-sa!" Hilja trilled. "I've come to see your new table. I heard you have it. And what a glorious day. Well, I can see what you're doing," she said, eyeing the piles of wash. "And a fine day it is for it, too. A nice breeze for drying. But so much!"

"It's the neighbor's," Kaisa said, making an effort to lighten her humor. "I take in his wash once a week."

"That's good. It gives you a little more beyond the egg money. Now why don't you leave all this for a while and sit down with me and rest? Ooo- '' Hilja complained. "It's too warm for so much walking. And my feet hurt."

"Why wear a coat? It's summer yet. We haven't even had a frost.'' Reluctantly, Kaisa untied her apron strings and unrolled the sleeves of the tan housedress as she followed Hilja into the kitchen.

Hilja fell into one of the straight-backed chairs. "You're young yet, but soon enough you'll know.''

"You make yourself old before your time," Kaisa said, glancing up at the ticking clock. "What brings you so early? It's not even eight o'clock.'' Kaisa scurried into the pantry for the tall enamel coffee pot. Now that Hilja was inside, she had no choice but to make coffee.

"Your new table!" Hilja exclaimed. She lifted a corner of the pungent oil cloth to admire the veneered top and stooped to examine the claw-footed pedestal. Clucking her tongue in approval, she said, "Soap labels?''

"Doing Pottles' wash I use a lot more soap." Despite all that had been on her mind, Kaisa experienced a glimmer of pleasure in Hilja's praise for the new table. For years, Kaisa had admired the tables in the homes of others and now, at last, she had one just as fine, if not finer, in her own home.

"Anni Seilonen got a little desk with soap labels. But I think you've seen it. In her parlor. It has a mirror at the top and two shelves for books. It's very nice. But this table— I've never seen one so fine. High tone, I'd say!''

More disposed now towards hospitality, Kaisa bustled into the pantry as Hilja talked on about the warm weather and the good corn crops. The tin clattered as Kaisa reached into it for some flat rye cookies. She then sliced into yesterday's *nisu*, arranging the cardamom-flavored bread on a little glass plate. She carried the cookies and sweet bread into the kitchen, setting them on the table alongside the sugar bowl and the fat green bowl of spoons, and then hurried out to the milk house for a pitcher of cream.

"Today is the day, isn't it?'' Hilja asked, raising one eyebrow, when Kaisa returned with the rich yellow cream. "The day Matti becomes a citizen of this country?''

Kaisa stiffened.

"What an honor," Hilja continued, apparently not noticing the change in climate, "to become a citizen of the United States of America. I only wish my husband had. But it's too late now. A joyous day it must be for you!"

Kaisa grimaced.

"Not joyous?"

"Not joyous at all!"

"Oh— I suppose you thought to go back to Finland?" Hilja flicked her thick fingers at Kaisa. "Everyone does. But no one goes back. And why should they? There's nothing there anymore. Only unrest. And hunger. The Tzar has our little country by the throat. Can't you remember the hard times? Grinding the bark of the pine tree to make bread? Do you want to do that again?"

"My mother and sisters are there!" Kaisa snapped. Hilja Kyllönen. Why had she come? Kaisa whisked back into the pantry for cups and saucers. She stopped for an angry moment to stare out the little window. The sheets on the clothesline flapped wetly in the breeze. Beyond the half-full line were the blue hills.

"Well, bring them here," Hilja said from the kitchen. "You're working and can afford to send them tickets. And now that you're citizens, it will be easy to bring relatives."

"They don't want to come." The everyday white cups chinked against the saucers as she set them on the table.

"As far as I'm concerned, I'm just as happy to be here in this country," Hilja sniffed. "Here we have everything. That nice comfortable house my husband left me. My boy takes good care of me. Plenty to eat. All the coffee and sugar I want."

"Coffee and sugar aren't everything." Kaisa snatched the coffee pot from the stove, not even letting the grounds settle.

"And you'll change your name, I heard. That is a wise thing. These days it goes easier for the Finn who is smart enough to change the name. That way the Yankees never know if you're from another country or not."

"That's ridiculous. All they have to do is look. And listen."

"Yes, but a man like Matti— He has a good way with

people. He'll make good with a new name."

"If he makes good," Kaisa blurted, unable to check the
words that flew from her mouth, "he'll make good without
me!" Kaisa gulped the steaming coffee, so hot that it scalded
her tongue and throat. She knew better than to keep talking
to Hilja Kyllönen. Within hours, her troubles would be news
all over Edom. Hilja had but started for the day. However,
because Kaisa's tongue had loosened with anger, it couldn't
be stopped. "If Matti changes the name, I will be Hannula
again! And then who knows what I will decide to do?"

Hilja gasped, fanning her broad face with her hand. And
then, as though they had been speaking of such things all
along, she leaned close to Kaisa's ear and whispered, "I
hear there's going to be another little one in the Mustonen
family. Can you imagine? The poor woman. And he drinks
so much. Why, last week— "

"Each child is a gift."

"Perhaps if you— "

"But I haven't!" Kaisa stood, smoothing down the front of
her shapeless housedress. "George Pottle expects his washing back tonight. I have work to do."

"Well!" Hilja spluttered. And then she said it again,
"Well!" But she did shrug into her thick black coat.

Hilja marched from the dooryard, her stride announcing
that she had purpose.

Kaisa was annoyed with herself that she had allowed
Hilja to learn how she felt about the name change. After all,
in the scheme of life, it was probably but a small thing. And
now it was too late.

Her anger huge, Kaisa attacked the diminishing mound of
clothes and, within no time, the line behind the house sagged.

Unable to stop, now that she had started, Kaisa dipped a
rag into a bucket of hot water, rubbed it with yellow soap,
and began to scrub woodwork—around the windows and
doors, along the mopboards and wainscoting, the shelves and
cupboards in the pantry. When that chore was through,
she mixed more hot water with vinegar and washed windows,
inside and out, in the kitchen and sitting room, the tiny back
room, the single window in the pantry, and even the wavy
panes in the woodshed.

That Hilja Kyllönen! Her only reason for coming had been to give her tongue something to waggle about. And knowing Hilja, by now she had already stopped at Mustonen's and was well on her way to Laurila's.

Kaisa then scrubbed the floors.

When the clothes were dry, Kaisa put two heavy flatirons on the stove to heat and brought in the huge load of fresh wash from the line. She smacked an iron over the wrinkled clothes, raising the scent of hot material. When one iron cooled, she banged it back on the stove, grabbing for the other.

The stack of crisp, folded clothes grew on the table until, at last, the basket was empty.

The shadows were growing longer. It was time for milking. Before she left the kitchen, though, she put a pot of wheat porridge on the back of the stove to cook.

She walked quickly enough, a long willow stick in hand, despite the weariness that was overtaking her. The two black and white Holsteins waited by the gate. The third, the same brown cow that always managed to be where she shouldn't, munched among the alders beyond the lower meadow.


That morning, the train had arrived at the county seat exactly on schedule, 8:47. Since the court appointment was not until 10:00, Matti had ample time to stroll the quiet elm-lined streets to the post office to mail Kaisa's letter to Finland.

It was in front of the drugstore where Matti had stopped for a nickel's worth of peppermints that he met Jaakko Paananen. Jaakko had become a citizen himself two years before, changing his name to Jack Paine. Not that Matti ever thought about him with the Yankee name. He called him Jaakko, the same as before.

As the two men walked to the post office, the warm sun on their shoulders, past the great double doors to the savings bank, the spreading elm tree in the square with the watering trough underneath, the false-fronted dry goods store, Jaakko brimmed with advice on how to speak to the judge in order that all would go well. And since he was a man of experience, he even knew how Matti could save two dollars on the lawyer's fee.

After Jaakko had spent some time boasting about the benefits of the new Yankee name, Matti asked, "Have you ever had any regrets about changing your name?"

"Never!" he said, as they waited for two automobiles to pass.

"But when you think about it," Matti mused, watching a farm wagon piled high with corn squeak past, "that is all a man ever has to pass on to his son, a good name. That was all my father had to leave me. My oldest brother got the bit of land. I got the name. But it was a good name. No tarnish to it."

"Horse manure! What difference does a name make?"

"I was wondering," Matti continued, "if to change it would make a difference."

"What's the matter with you? Why waste your time thinking about foolishness? Change your name. Life will be easier. Listen to *me*. I know."

While Matti stood in line at the iron grill in the post office, Jaakko, his hands clasped behind his back, waited in front of the Wanted posters.

Together they strolled along the narrow dirt paths of the park and lounged side-by-side on a stiff slat bench next to the spouting fountain. Sunlight sparkled through the shade of the still-green maple trees onto the spraying water.

And although the conversation had veered to the benefits of planting winter rye, Matti again mentioned what was foremost on his mind. "Do you ever feel odd with that name?" he asked, watching a woman in a feathered hat and hobbled skirt mince past across the park.

"Never!" Jaakko insisted, stretching his legs before him and hooking his thumbs beneath his suspenders. "Oh, perhaps a little at first— When I wrote to my relatives back in Finland, I had trouble writing the new name. But— I don't write to them much anyway," he shrugged.

As Matti waited for Mr. Mason, he paced back and forth in front of the red brick courthouse, shunning the other immigrants waiting on the granite steps. When at last Mr. Mason rounded the corner, Matti dashed to meet him.

"Kilponen be a good name!" Matti spluttered, the English

words tumbling from his mouth. "I no change. Kilponen be a good name!"

*****

It was late that afternoon when Matti got off the train in Edom. He carried a beautifully embossed white certificate and a small red, white and blue silk flag. The nickel's worth of peppermints bulged in a paper sack in his pocket.

The pride he felt knew no bounds. It seemed that he walked taller. Straighter. Anyone seeing him could surely tell that the day had been a momentous one.

He wasted no time in getting to the livery to pick up his horse and wagon. On the road home, he snapped the reins over the horse's back whenever its pace slowed.

As soon as he was within sight of the little farm, however, Matti brought the horse to a slow trudge. It would never do to make a show of excitement. Without even a glance towards the house, Matti eased the express into its spot next to the barn, led the big brown horse to its stall, hung up the harnesses and collar, got a bucket of slippery oats.

Dangling the silk flag and embossed certificate, Matti, seemingly unconcerned, ambled through the woodshed with its sparkling windows, into the spotlessly clean kitchen. Evening sunlight shone bright over the long colorful rag runners on the shiny floor. Not a speck of dust nor crumb was in sight. The good smell of porridge and bread toasting in the frying pan teased his nostrils, making him realize that many hours had passed since he had last eaten.

Kaisa stood by the stove, stirring the porridge.

Seeing her stiffness, Matti no longer felt quite as tall. And he wasn't at all sure what to say. "I— " he began, the red, white and blue flag in his hand drooping.

Kaisa bustled past him into the pantry and came back with a basket of clean brown eggs.

"I'm a citizen now," he said, irked that she was whisking about, paying no heed to him.

She cracked an egg into the frying pan and broke the yolk with a fork.

"See. Here is the certificate. It says I am a citizen. I can vote."

Kaisa barely glanced at the white paper Matti held. Instead, she cracked another egg.

"I— " Matti's face flushed.

Her back to her husband, Kaisa slid the slices of crusty browned bread onto the eggs.

"I told— " Matti again tried.

Still Kaisa busied herself, spooning water from a cup over the crisp crusts, the droplets sizzling in the hot pan.

What a stubborn woman she was! Pretending not to hear. Her indifference was enough to infuriate any man. Matti reached out for her, twirling her about by her narrow shoulders. He gripped her with both hands, shouting into her face. "Teo-dorr Rrroo-se-velte's father didn't change his name. And look. PRESIDENT! Two times."

Kaisa blinked in surprise. Matti looked ridiculous. Scowling. His face red. Raising his voice about Theodore Roosevelte's father.

"And PRESIDENT again! You'll see," he raged, shaking her hard.

Was Matti saying that he hadn't changed the name? That the name was still Kilponen? A good Finnish name? Why, of course— And then Kaisa started to giggle, unable to stop as he shook her. "Yes!" she gasped. "Kilponen! It is a good name. Is— Isn't it?"

Sheepishly, Matti relaxed, shoving his hands into his pockets, rambling towards the front windows and back again. "Here," he said, thrusting the white paper sack at her. "Peppermints. You always say you like peppermints."

Kaisa peered into the bag. "Peppermints?" she asked shyly, reaching out to touch her husband's calloused hand. "I do like peppermints. But let's sit down. Supper is ready."

# SAFFRON BUNS

1914

It had been Christmas in Finland the first time Kaisa Kilponen had a saffron bun. Although, at the time, she hadn't known what it was that flavored the sweet bread so delicately.

She had been in the service of a landowner, so wealthy that he had three hired girls tending his cows and making the rich butter and cheese which were taken to market. The lady of the house, wrapped snugly in bright blue woolens trimmed in brown fur, herself carried a filigreed plate piled high with soft golden buns to the barn. The little breads were shaped in four-petaled clusters, and in each of the swirling petals was a plump, brown raisin. Kaisa had been only thirteen at the time, but she had known to curtsey.

Taking tiny bites of the sweet roll in order to savor it, Kaisa had stood just out of sight inside the barn door as the lady and her three chattering children rode off for holiday visits in a shiny sleigh, all of them tucked under a thick bearskin rug. The bells on the horses' harnesses jangled, and the soft snow sprayed up behind them. Kaisa had watched until they were only a speck disappearing into the distant pine forest.

The second time she had had a saffron bun, it had also been
Christmas. But this time in America. When at last the
women, after the men and children, could also sit for coffee
in the crowded church hall, Kaisa helped herself to one of the
few remaining buns on the platter. It was shaped in a four-
petaled cluster with a brown raisin in each petal. "Who
made these?" she asked.

Hilja Kyllönen, who always knew what everyone brought,
nodded her head towards the well-dressed stranger among
the Mikkonens. "She did. She's their relative. From New
York City." Hilja leaned closer. "They say she's very wealthy.
Married to a Yankee."

"What do you think she used for flavoring?" Kaisa asked,
studying the bun as if for a clue. "It's not cardamom. It's
different."

"You mean to say you don't know what it is?" Hilja said,
bobbing her head so that her jowls wobbled. "Anyone should
know that it's saffron!"

"Saffron?"

"That's what I said. Saffron. Don't you know that in
Finland it's often used by the gentry at Christmas? But it's
expensive. Very. Of course, someone of *her* means— "

Kaisa took another small bite. She could almost smell
the sweet earthy scent of the cow stalls where she had been in
service at age thirteen.

After that, a Christmas hadn't gone by that Kaisa didn't
talk about saffron buns. More than anything else, she wanted
to make saffron buns at Christmas.

She sent Matti for saffron when he went to the Edom
General Store in town, but neither Amos Cole nor his wife
Sally had even heard of it. When he went to the county seat
on business, Matti asked for it in the drug store. The druggist,
a kind and patient man who valued his Finnish customers
and stocked cardamom just for them, explained that he
couldn't carry saffron because of its price. Once Matti even
tried to get it in Lewiston, but the French-speaking clerk
didn't understand Matti and Matti didn't understand the
clerk, so he left empty-handed. But still Kaisa talked about

saffron buns. She always hoped that the wealthy relative
of the Mikkonens would return, but she never did.


It was in the early fall that the Nurmi brothers, Sulo and
Eino, decided to go back to Finland for a visit. It seemed
that almost every Finnish family had a message or a letter
to send, a little piece of handiwork wrapped in white paper or
a photograph in a brown envelope. When Matti gave Sulo
his letters, he also asked, in secret, for a favor.

"On your return through Helsinki, get some saffron for my
wife. All she can think about at Christmas is saffron buns.
If she could only make some, she might stop that foolish talk."
He put a shiny dollar into Sulo's hand. "Just a little. I hear
it's expensive."

At the end of November, the Nurmi brothers returned
from their long voyage and went from house to house, this
time leaving behind a message or a letter, a piece of handiwork wrapped in white paper, or a photograph in a brown
envelope. And at each house, the two brothers were eagerly
welcomed over the coffee table.

"But what is it?" Kaisa asked. To her it looked like a
medicine in the corked glass vial.

"It's what you've been yammering about for the past
five years," Matti blustered. "What's the matter, woman,
that you don't even know what it is you want? It's saffron,
of course!"

"Saffron?" The word burst from her lips in a little puff
of air. "Saffron? Why, I've never seen it before— I had no
idea what it was like. I thought it must be something like
cardamom."

"It's from Helsinki," Eino boasted. "From the very store
where the gentry buy their goods."

"Imagine!" Kaisa couldn't stop smiling. "Imagine!"

"All you need to use is a pinch," Sulo said, squeezing his
forefinger and thumb to show her. "And then rub it to break
it up. That's what they said in Helsinki."

"That's right," Eino added. "You don't need much.
There's plenty here for one big batch or two medium batches

they said. Just make *nisu* like you always do and drop the
saffron in the hot milk. But break it up!'' He too squeezed
his forefinger and thumb.

Overwhelmed with emotion, Kaisa hurried into the pantry
for another *nisu*. "Eat! Eat!'' she urged, wanting the two
travelers to feel welcome.

Matti beamed. "I'm the one who asked them. I knew what
you'd want.''

When Kaisa was sure that neither Sulo nor Eino was
watching, she passed behind her husband and patted him on
the shoulder. She then stood next to the stove as the men had
their coffee.

"Just remember. Pinch it to break it up,'' Sulo again
reminded.


A light snow drifted from the cold gray sky the morning of
Christmas Eve. It was still early when Kaisa, already through
her regular chores, stretched on tiptoe for the big green
bowl from the tall pantry shelf. In it she dissolved yeast in
warm water.

As the creamy top milk scalded, Kaisa stood right beside
the stove. She wasn't going to leave it for a second, knowing
it would boil the minute her back was turned.

Her fingers nervously tapped out half the contents of the
tiny vial into her palm. After much thought, she had decided
to use only half and save the rest. Pinching the fragile threads
between her thumb and forefinger—just the way the Nurmi
brothers had told her to—she dropped the saffron into the
warmed milk. Each dark red particle burst into a swirl of
yellow-orange color, exuding a faint exotic scent. She smiled
in happy satisfaction as she rubbed her orange-stained
fingers with a rough cloth.

Into the milk and yeast, she added a scoop of sugar, threw
a pinch of salt, poured some melted butter, cracked five fresh
eggs and then stirred it all with the long-handled wooden
spoon Matti had carved last winter during a February blizzard.
At last! Saffron buns for Christmas. *"Terve oi Joulu, iltamme
armain. . . .* Welcome, O Christmas, evening beloved. . . .''

The words of the hymn danced through her heart.

Sitting on a straight-backed kitchen chair with the bowl snug between her knees, she worked in the flour. Each time she added another handful, a fine mist puffed into her face, powdering her nose and eyebrows. She mixed the sticky dough with her strong hand, kneading her fingers through the yellow mass. She hummed as she worked. Her special gift to the congregation of the Lutheran Church that night at the children's program would be the saffron buns. She added more flour, blowing the flying white dust away from her upper lip.

She left the dough to rise under a spotless white towel and started a rye-meal crust for a batch of rice pies. Two apple pies she had baked the day before sat on the pantry shelf. For a moment she wondered whether she should make something else. It would be terrible if there weren't enough.

As she swept the floors, upstairs and down, Kaisa remembered the five pairs of brown mittens and hats trimmed with red she had knitted earlier in the fall for the Mustonen children. Their father had taken to liquor so heavily that there was never anything left over for the four little girls and the boy who was nothing more than a baby in diapers. Last winter her heart had wrenched every time she had seen them looking so cold. Their noses running. If only she and Matti had had children— She sighed. Well, this winter, at least, they would all have warm mittens and hats. She had taken care of that. Somewhere was that large piece of white butcher paper she had saved to wrap them. Now, where had she put it?

Kaisa always enjoyed the Christmas tree at church. She loved the white candles and the pretty bits of brightly colored paper tied to the tree. She knew that some of the families put up trees in their homes as the Yankees did, but she and Matti celebrated Christmas in the church. That, after all, was what it was all about. *"Terve oi Joulu, iltamme armain . . . ."* The opening stanza ran through her head.

As the buns baked, she waited beside the oven door with a folded towel in her hand, ready to switch the two pans from top to bottom. Snowflakes swirled outside the window. The warm kitchen filled with the sweet yeasty aroma of bread baking.

Just then, she heard Matti bellow from outside and saw a flash of black and white past the windows. Something was wrong! She hurried to the door. The heifer was loose. How had it gotten out at this time of year? Cows! Always making for problems.

"Get her!" Matti shouted as he came around the corner of the barn. "Turn her around!"

Reaching for the worn broom beside the door, Kaisa dashed after the heifer, trying to turn her before she got to the road. The skittish animal wavered on an icy patch and started for the empty snow-covered field behind the house.

"You foolish cow!" Kaisa shouted, waving her broom. "Get back where you belong."

"Stay there. I'll get some grain. Don't move," Matti ordered, disappearing into the barn while Kaisa hovered near the nervous animal.

Kaisa shivered. Her long hair, pulled back into a tight little bun, left her neck exposed to the cold snow. She hadn't had time to put anything over her shoulders. She hunched her arms around the broom. The heifer veered again towards the road, and Kaisa dashed into its path, turning it around.

Carrying a dented bucket in one hand and a heaping handful of grain in the other, Matti coaxed the awkward, leggy animal back towards the barn door.

Suddenly Kaisa remembered. "Aghh— !" she shrieked, nearly falling on the ice as she headed for the kitchen. "The buns! The buns!"

Black smoke rolled from the oven door. The saffron buns, that had been lovingly twirled into four-petaled clusters, were nothing more than charred black lumps.

With the towel she yanked the top pan from the oven. Cows! Stupid animals. Nothing but trouble. As she reached for the bottom pan, her hand grazed the edge of the hot rack. For a second she felt nothing, but then a searing pain shot up her arm. Tears welled in her eyes.

Her mouth set, she gripped the pan and dashed across the kitchen to heave it with all her strength out the open door.

At just that moment Matti was picking his way over the slippery pathway back into the house. He stopped in his

snowy tracks when not only a pan but a panful of black buns
whizzed past his head. As the hot baking sheet hit the snow,
it buckled and sank out of sight.

Later, when the acrid smell had disappeared from the
kitchen and Kaisa had had two cups of coffee, she tied on her
woolen kerchief and went outside to retrieve her baking tins.
In disgust, she kicked a little black lump, one of the remains
of her Christmas buns, deeper into the snow.

Once again, she dissolved yeast in warm water. And once
again, she waited for a pan of hot milk to scald, not taking her
eyes from it for a second. And she held her breath when
she spilled out the contents of the little stoppered vial, the
last of the red-orange saffron.

Tiptoeing around the cloth-covered green bowl, she stayed
near as the dough rose. At last the mound crept up over the
rim. She formed the buns, twisting the dough into dainty
four-petaled clusters, and spaced them precisely on the two
baking sheets. And then, into each petal, she placed a soft,
plump, brown raisin.

Thrusting his head through the kitchen door, Matti judged
that it was at last safe to go in. But he knew better than to
say a word about there not being a thing set out for his coffee.
Instead he clattered down the wobbly cellar stairs and came
back with two apples, firm but spotted northern spies, and
sat at the table to peel them as though he would want nothing
more than apples with his coffee.

"Now you finally have your saffron buns for Christmas,"
he said a little too jovially as he poked one of the peeled
apple quarters into his mouth.

"Don't talk to me!" Kaisa snapped, her face flushed from
the heat of the woodstove. "And why don't you find something to do. I don't want to be bothered with anything more.
And clean up those apple peels!"

Matti started to protest her bad humor but then thought
the better of it. He scooped up the pieces of apple and the
stringy peelings and thumped across the kitchen to fumble
into his coat and hat. "I'll go check the *sauna*," he said, the
door banging behind him.

The heat rushed against her face as she peeked into the
oven. The buns on the rack had swollen nicely and were

browning. Those on the oven floor had browned evenly on
their bottoms. She shifted the pans and closed the door.
Shutting her eyes, she wiped her apron hem across her moist
forehead.

She didn't wait for long before looking again. The buns
were just as they should be—puffy, golden four-petaled
clusters. Two pans of perfect saffron buns.

As they cooled, she mixed a sugary glaze to brush over
the tops so they'd glisten and, resisting the temptation to
sample even one, wrapped the buns in clean towels to keep
them soft.


In winter, *sauna* was usually warmed only on a Saturday,
but on Christmas Eve, though it might be a Tuesday or a
Friday, there was an early *sauna*. For no Finn would honor
the Christ Child's birth unless he was cleansed in body and
spirit. So in mid-afternoon, when the kitchen was at last in
order, Matti and Kaisa had a hot *sauna* and dressed in their
best for the Christmas Eve service.

Into her big wicker basket, Kaisa placed the five sets of
hats and mittens wrapped in white butcher paper, a small
bundle of greeting cards with the names of parishioners
written in a neat hand across the envelopes, two apple pies,
five rice pies and a big jug of day-old top milk for coffee.
Last of all, she made a space for the saffron buns, piled nicely
on a rose-tinted glass plate.

Carrying the covered basket between them, they walked
through the new snow to church. The storm had passed, and
although there was no moon, the night was not dark. The
bright fresh snow softened the angles of rocks and fence
posts, making the familiar unfamiliar. Kaisa breathed deeply.
The spirit of Christmas had returned to her heart.

They were among the first to arrive. While Matti stoked
the woodstoves, both upstairs and down, Kaisa unpacked the
basket at the work table in the quiet kitchen. From there she
went to the tables in the dining hall, setting them with the
heavy coffee mugs and bowls of sugar spoons. The children's
table had already been set with fat round oranges and boxes of

ribbon candy decorated with pictures of the three wise men, each box with the name of a child printed across the top.

As others arrived with their plates of Christmas foods, greeting cards and perhaps a small gift or two, the kitchen and dining hall filled with their laughter and chatter. Erkki Seilonen, who seemed to fancy himself as Father Christmas, lugged a wooden box, heavy with bottles of colorful soda—orange, raspberry, lemon-lime. Kaisa, spying him across the crowded hall, hurried to greet him and together they put a bottle at each child's place.

At last Kaisa squeezed into one of the middle pews on the women's side next to Hilja. The tow-headed children in the front pews were so shiny and clean they seemed to have been polished. Only the Mustonen girls looked as though they needed a hot *sauna*. Kaisa clucked to herself. Just because you're poor doesn't mean you can't be clean. After all, we're all poor. She fingered the corner of her pocket-sized hymnal. Slender white candles flickered on the tall bushy fir tree in front of the curved altar rail.

The last wheezing notes of the opening hymn faded, the signal for the children to begin.

Tiina Piirainen, swaying to a sing-song rhythm, recited her lines.

Matti Leino forgot the Bible verse.

Riitva and Elna Mustonen, their hair stringy and their dresses grimy, mumbled to the floor.

But six-year old Antti Laurila stood so boldly and spoke so clearly that even the old men in the back pew heard every word. Kaisa glanced to the men's side at Tuomo, swollen with a father's pride. Her eyes blurred. If she could have a son, she'd want one just like Antti Laurila. His round cheeks were flushed with excitement and his blue eyes danced with mischief. Children! How they sparkled at Christmas.

With the rest of the congregation, Kaisa put her whole heart into the final hymn *"Terve oi Joulu"*.

Amidst a noisy chatter, Erkki Seilonen passed the greeting cards out and, last of all, the gifts—a fancy box of handkerchiefs for someone's uncle, a book of Bible stories for a son or daughter, stockings and mittens for the children. Kaisa bit her lip as the Mustonen girls opened their packages. Helga, the youngest of the girls, pulled the warm brown hat trimmed in red over her limp dark blond hair and smiled so prettily at her older sister that Kaisa wished she had made more.

Old Veikko Kuvaja in the back pew stood to mutter his own Christmas message. As he droned on, the children whispered and fidgeted and two-by-two and three-by-three slipped down the center aisle to go downstairs to peek at their Christmas table.

The women, too, drifted down to the kitchen to tie on their long aprons and uncover the braids and fancy rings of sweet breads, the frosted buns, the apple pies, the rice pies, the cakes, the sugar cookies.


With a pitcher of cream in her hand, Kaisa peered over the crowded tables. Everyone seemed to have enough. Certainly there was plenty of food. She looked for her plate of buns. They weren't on Pastori Halme's table. Nor were there any on the other men's table. And there wasn't a single one on the long children's table either. They must not have been put out. With all the other food, the saffron buns must have been overlooked.

"My buns— " Kaisa said to Hilja, as she picked through the clutter of towels and baskets on the work table. "I can't seem to find them."

"Aren't they out on the tables?"

"I didn't see them."

"Maybe you forgot to bring them."

"Of course I brought them! They were right on top."

Together the two women made the rounds of the crowded tables. But they didn't find the plate of saffron buns.

"Did you check the kitchen?" Elvi Laurila asked, overhearing them.

So once again the kitchen was searched. They didn't find the buns, but Elvi did find Kaisa's rose-tinted glass plate beneath a small stack of heavy white church plates.

"Now that's the strangest thing," Kaisa said. "The plate is here, but what happened to the buns?"

"It looks to me as though the men have already eaten them," Elvi said.

"So fast?" Kaisa's heart sank. She hand't even sampled one. And she had wanted the women to try them as well. She smiled weakly, holding fast to her disappointment.

Easing past the jumble of chairs at the children's table, Kaisa noticed that little Antti and his two cousins Helmeri and Heikki had barely touched their bottles of raspberry soda. Fat sugar cookies sat on their plates. And not only that, the boxes of ribbon candy had not even been opened.

"What's the matter, boys?" Kaisa asked, patting Antti's fine straight hair. "Are you too excited to eat?"

Tears welled in Antti's blue eyes. "No, Aunt Kaisa," he squeaked. (Antti always called Kaisa "aunt".) "But Father is going to strap us!" With that he buried his face in his small arms against the side of the table and started to sob.

"But why? What are you talking about?" Kaisa asked. The heaving shoulders distressed her, for a child's tears were enough to bring tears to her eyes as well.

"It's because Antti ate all the buns!" Helmeri blurted. "That's why he's crying. He ate all the buns."

"You ate some too!" Antti retorted.

"But you started!"

"What? What buns?" But of course Kaisa already knew. "And Heikki?" she asked.

Heikki didn't say a word. He just hung his head, so fair, it was almost white.

For a second Kaisa stood, gripping the back of Antti's chair, unable to speak. But then she said, not hiding the sharpness in her voice, "You three little boys ate all those buns? There were so many! How could three little boys eat so many buns?" She felt her face growing red. Her eyes wanted to cloud. The saffron buns? Three little boys? ALL HER SAFFRON BUNS?

She looked down at the frightened white faces and, fleetingly, a strange thrill ran through her. She wanted to lash out at each one of them.

But when Antti began to shudder with big wet sobs, she softened. She knew *she* wouldn't be the one to scold them. She couldn't.

"Now! Now!" she whispered, her hands fluttering help-lessly. "It's Christmas. Don't cry. Those buns were for you. For you children."

Antti's voice quavered, "But Father— "

She shook her head. "I'm the one who brought those buns. They were for YOU!" She looked down at the three and then glanced over her shoulder at Tuomo, deep in talk with Matti. It was, after all, only a batch of *nisu*. She dropped a gentle hand to Antti's small shoulder and, as though it were an afterthought, asked, "And how were they? Were they very good?"

"Kaisa! Kaisa!" Hilja shrilled over the children. "We can have our coffee now."

Kaisa patted each of the three heads, the hair soft against her rough hand.

"Your buns?" Hilja asked. "Did you find them? After so much talk about saffron buns, I want to try one, too."

Kaisa fumbled with the button on her jacket. "The men— " she shrugged.

"So good they're gone already?" Hilja shook her head in disbelief.


The night air was still and cold. Stars shone brightly in the cloudless sky. As they walked, Matti carried the basket, nearly empty except for the rose-tinted glass plate, two pie tins, a left-over rice pie and some folded towels. He put his free arm tentatively around his wife's shoulder.

"I didn't even have a one of those buns of yours," he said.

"No? Well, neither did I. I guess they were too good. They went that fast."

The snow squeaked pleasantly underfoot. For an instant, Kaisa once again stood just inside the barn door, savoring a soft saffron bun. The lady of the house in her fur-trimmed coat and her three children rode off in a big sleigh, the snow flying.

"I think," Kaisa at last said, "that I prefer cardamom. It's much simpler."

# BERRYING

1916

Footsteps, followed by a hacking cough, sounded in the spare room above. Kaisa Kilponen and her husband Matti both glanced up to the smoke-darkened plaster of the ceiling. Kaisa jabbed the sewing needle into the worn brown trousers she was mending. "Why did you bring her here?" she whispered sharply.

Matti, with *The County Observer* spread out on the round kitchen table before him, said, "You know that she didn't have anyplace to go. And she almost died from the influenza. You can see that she is weak. And she said she wanted to be around womenfolk."

Matti returned to the newspaper, his finger underscoring the line of print, his lips mouthing the English words. Only when he had finished the column did he look at his wife and say, "It's just for a few weeks. Until Nestori gets back from the quarries at the coast. There's work there now. It says so. Right here."

Kaisa sat stiffly, her arms crossed, the sewing untouched on her lap. She stared across the kitchen at the rain streaking the windows in the gray dusk.

"You don't think she could stay in the woods alone, do you?
Not the way she is now. Remember— The Bible says, 'Do
unto . . .' "

"They're not married!"

"They're as good as married. All these years."

At Kaisa's feet, a coffee-colored dog named Karhu
stretched and then nestled his huge muzzle onto his wide
front paws. Kaisa looked down at the dog and broke the
thread with her teeth. She folded the trousers neatly into
thirds and dropped her thimble into the cigar box she used
for sewing notions. "And what if he doesn't come back?"
she asked, her mouth tight. "Do we just keep Lena the way
we kept Karhu?" She didn't trust that the bent, red-whisk-
ered man with the odd twitch to his eye would return. When
Matti had brought them home through the rain that afternoon,
*Komia* Nestori, or Pretty Nestori, had dropped Leena's
meager bundle, wrapped in a wet gray shawl, and had spun
to go. With the dog barking beside her, Kaisa had reluctantly
called out to him to come in for coffee, but Nestori hadn't
bothered to turn back. "He probably has no intention of
coming for her! He's going to take his money and go away.
To Canada. Or Minnesota."

"He'll come," Matti yawned, reaching for the heavy silver
watch in his pocket and checking it against the clock that
ticked between the front windows. "Put the dog out, and
let's go to bed," he said, picking up the lamp.

Again, there was the hacking cough from above.


Over the years, Matti had spoken of Leena Hakola in such
admiring terms that Kaisa sometimes wondered whether or
not he carried a spark for her. It didn't seem to matter to
Matti that she was skinny, or that her gapped teeth were
stained from years of chewing tobacco, or that her frowzy
hair was never pulled back into the neat bun that all modest
Finnish women wore. The two never stopped talking. It
seemed that they had already resurrected every Yankee,
every Canadian, every Finn who had ever worked in the
lumber camp. Every meal Leena had cooked. Every dollar

lost to gambling and whiskey. Every accident. Every hard time. Every good time.

Leena's eyes snapped and laughter rattled from her when she recalled some incident. With Leena, Matti quipped in a way he never did with Kaisa. Only when Leena, with a dingy handkerchief to her mouth and her eyes swollen with tears, broke down in a spell of coughing, did they stop.

No one could say that Leena didn't try to please Kaisa. With the first light of dawn, Leena was up, poking kindling at Kaisa as she started the morning fire. When the coffee was ready, Leena sat between Matti and Kaisa slurping steaming coffee from her saucer just as Matti did from his. Kaisa could barely taste her own coffee for listening to Leena's noisy inhalations. Although, to tell the truth, Matti had been drinking his coffee as noisily for years, and Kaisa had barely noticed.

Whenever Kaisa went into the barn to do her morning chores, Leena was there. Always talking. The cows balked at her strange touch and were skittish when she coughed. The usually docile animals jumped and kicked, and milk spilled.

Despite the many years of praise Kaisa had received for her crusty bread and tasty stews, Leena offered up advice from her years of experience as a cook in the lumber camps. "When I make it in the camp— " she'd begin, so that the blood would boil in Kaisa's head.

As soon as a meal was over, Leena would dash to the slate sink, insisting that she would be the one to wash dishes. "Why don't you go rest," Kaisa would say as she hovered close by, watching Leena haphazardly dip greasy plates, forks and knives into water that was barely warm. And afterwards, Leena would grab the broom to flick at the crumbs around the table. When Leena, finally exhausted, did go upstairs to lie down, Kaisa would stealthily pick the dishes out of the pantry cupboard to wash them again in water that steamed and turned the hands red. And then she'd wield the broom with a sore vengeance, attacking the four corners of the roomy kitchen, moving the woodbox aside to get every woodchip and splinter, and rolling the long rag runners to carry outside and beat so that not a speck of dust dared linger.

The more Leena tried, the worse it got with Kaisa so that she became quieter and quieter. And the quieter Kaisa grew, the more Matti tried to make up the difference with Leena.

Leena no longer chewed tobacco, but she did now smoke a pipe. Several times a day, she lit her pipe, dribbling shreds of tobacco and leaving behind the heady scent of Prince Albert.

"I don't like the way it smells," Kaisa complained to her husband as she scooped up bits of tobacco from the table. "And look at this mess!"

Matti took Leena aside and suggested that she not smoke inside the house. After that, Leena smoked on the front stoop with the dog Karhu beside her, thumping his stub of a tail as she rubbed his back.

Kaisa, seeing how the dog seemed to be taking to Leena, sometimes poked in the pantry for a bit of gristly meat or a scrap of bread. And then, with a good deal of noise, she rattled the dog's tin dish, watching in satisfaction as he greedily dashed to her. At such times, though, Leena seemed to take no notice.

When the dog, with the look of a scruffy brown bear, had appeared at their door one morning, Kaisa, not heeding Matti's caution, had given it the remainder of her porridge mixed with a raw egg and milk. "If the dog wants to stay," she had said, "we'll keep it for a cow dog. All the farms have cow dogs. And since he resembles a bear, let's call him *Karhu.*"

Karhu, however, proved to be worthless with cows. His barking drove them in the opposite direction of the barn, and at midday when they should have been comfortably chewing their cuds in the shade of a tree, the dog would excite them. Matti threatened to get rid of the dog, but Kaisa wouldn't hear of it.

But one evening as they ate supper, Kaisa suddenly said, "Maybe we should do away with that good-for-nothing dog. He's not earning *his* keep around here!"

Leena looked up in surprise.

Matti ignored his wife.

It was a fine August morning when Matti told the two
women about the blueberries. Knowing how much Kaisa
enjoyed picking berries, he felt sure that Leena would be of the
same persuasion. And perhaps, he thought, with a few berries
to pick, Kaisa might slip into a more cheerful frame of mind.

"You know where I mean. On the ridge above Pottles',"
he said. And then to tempt his wife further, he added, "As
thick as— As grapes! They've never grown so plentifully."

"Leena, you stay here and rest," Kaisa said, her eyes
flashing with excitement. "It's a long walk. Too far for you.
And steep. You'll get tired if you go."

But Leena wouldn't hear of it. She wouldn't mind the
walk. She wanted to help. Going out into the sunshine would
be healthful. And she wouldn't get tired. And if she did get
tired, she would just sit down and rest. Look how much better
she was already after just a few weeks. Yes. She would go.
To keep Kaisa company.

"But going so far will make you cough— " Kaisa said.

"I don't cough so much now," Leena insisted. "I'll go
with you."

There was no convincing her otherwise.

"Oh, I almost forgot to tell you," Matti added, increasingly
hopeful that berrying would make Kaisa more agreeable.
"George Pottle has pastured his bull in that big field. You'll
have to go around. There's no trusting a bull."


As soon as the few morning duties were out of the way—
the dishes washed, the kitchen neat and tidy, a pot of beans
for supper baking in the oven—Kaisa collected two lard pails,
a cooking pot and a shiny milk bucket. Handing the two lard
pails to Leena, she set the larger containers on the table for
herself.

She filled a glass jug with hot milky coffee and slid it into an
old woolen stocking to keep it hot. From the crock on the
pantry shelf, she reached for a handful of rusks and grabbed
for two cracked white mugs. Putting all of these into a birch

bark pack which she shrugged over her shoulders, she pulled
a faded purple kerchief from the hook by the door and tied it
under her chin.

Matti was sharpening his scythe at the grindstone and
watched as the two women left the dooryard. Kaisa, with the
pack over her shoulders, carrying the cooking pot and milk
bucket, scurried two steps ahead of Leena. And behind
Leena, Karhu followed.

"I've never told you," Leena puffed, trying to keep pace
with Kaisa's stride, "that back in Finland, my aunt—that
would be my mother's sister—met her Maker because of a
bull. What a tragedy! It happened that she was taking her
nice little cow to her neighbor's for a little loving. You know
what I'm saying, eh? That bull had no idea when he saw my
aunt leading that cow that he should be grateful. There was
nothing left of Lempi *täti* they said. I never saw her myself.
But they told. me." And after a moment's reflection, she
added, "We won't go through that pasture, eh? We'll go
around. Just the way Matti said, eh?"

"If you're so worried, maybe you should go back."

"No! No! I'll help you pick berries. And we'll make a
blueberry soup. Nice and sweet, eh? But I won't go near
that bull!"

Kaisa's step quickened. Behind her, Leena walked faster.
The dog Karhu, with his black nose to the ground, wandered
off into the bushes.

"I see that you made beans this morning," Leena huffed.
"Sometime I'll make beans for you. Matti likes my beans.
In the lumbercamp, those men, they said, 'Leena!' they said.
'Leena, you make good beans.' "

Kaisa's lips tightened. She eyed a small white cloud.
"Matti *likes* my beans," she said, her feet wanting to fly.

But the faster Kaisa walked, the faster Leena walked, her
breathing becoming labored, the two lard pails clinking
unevenly.

"When I go back to Finland," Leena started, her voice
breathy, "I'll tell your people how you let me stay here. And
I'll go back in style, too. Maybe a new coat. A new shawl.
A new hat with flowers. And everyone will say, 'Leena,

Leena, you went to America, and now you're a rich woman.'
I'll tell everyone how you and Matti took care of me when I
was sick and Nestori went to find work in the quarry. I'll
go and take greetings to your mother and sisters. Now what
did you say their names are? Liisa and— ? And— ?" Leena
stopped to cough, her dirty handkerchief to her mouth.

"Liisa and Ani!" Kaisa snapped, turning to wait for Leena.
"And how do you think you'll get back to Finland? You don't
have that kind of money," Kaisa fumed. Even she had long
ago given up the idea of going back to her homeland.

They passed the stone wall that marked the line to George
Pottle's farm and soon came to the white house encircled with
a wide veranda and the steep-roofed barn with its pointed
cupola. Every time she passed George Pottle's house, Kaisa
wanted to peek in one of the curved front windows. Just to
see what was inside. She imagined it must be very fine.
Finer than she had ever seen. But the two women walked past
with perhaps even a little more haste.

"It's shorter if we go through," Kaisa said as they paused
to rest at the edge of the big field. Rich and green with lush
clover, it was a field large enough to feed a whole herd of
cattle. And all for one bull, Kaisa thought. What a good life
he leads. But where was he? She squinted, peering across
the pasture. Glancing at Leena from the corner of her eye,
she blurted, "Let's go," and jerked the heavy thick strands of
barbed wire apart.

"You heard what Matti said!" Leena cried, shrinking back
from the fence. He said to go around."

"*Voi*! *Voi*! How much time will we lose if we have to go
around?" Although earlier Kaisa had had no intention of
crossing through the field, she now felt that she wanted to
insist.

"Are we in so much of a hurry that we'll risk our lives?
Don't you see? Over there."

Even from where she stood, Kaisa could see that the black
bull was enormous. As a rule, she was sensible enough to
have a mighty respect for the power of such a creature.
But today, her annoyance with Leena made her tongue care-
less. "As though we couldn't go faster." However, with a

shrug, she headed for the steep tangled path that ran alongside the green pasture.

The dog Karhu, though, scooted under the barbed wire
into the thick clover.

"Come back!" Kaisa demanded. "Karhu!"

The dog turned to look.

"Come, Karhu— " Leena crooned.

But the coffee-colored dog sat, his stubby tail wagging.

"Leave him," Kaisa said, trudging up the narrow trail.
"If he thinks he's going to chase that bull, he'll learn fast
enough."

"Come, Karhu. Come— " Leena called again, slapping her
hands together invitingly. But then, she, too, hurried along.

The trail was far from smooth. Brushy growth, fallen logs,
and jutting rocks provided obstacles for each step. Flying
branches slapped Leena's cheek, and thorny brambles snarled
her hands.

At last though, Kaisa, and then Leena emerged from the
tangle of dark woods onto the bright sunny ledge. At their

feet were patches of blue amongst the gray rocks, for blue-berries grew everywhere, as abundantly as Matti had said.

Kaisa sighed.

Beyond were the roll and peaks of mountains to the west. Neat patchwork fields and farms dotted the distant hills. A lake, seemingly no larger than Kaisa's shoe, nestled in the green valley below. And there was the tiny village of Edom with two rising church steeples. Kaisa felt so close to God at the moment that her heart was suddenly sweet with goodness for Leena.

"Well!" Leena exclaimed, her face red from the climb. "Look at that! I've never seen so far. It's not as flat as in Finland. Maybe we can see where Nestori went, eh? And so many berries." And then she started to cough. But despite her hacking, she continued, "Remember in Finland? The berries were so small? One here. One there." She coughed, her eyes watering. "What work to fill the dish. But we did it. We had to. Times were so bad. My mother one time made porridge from wood shavings. And then from straw. What times they were! But we picked berries when we could. Remember?" she said, coughing.

"Remember? Of course, I remember!"

Kaisa had always loved berrying. Loved to feel the sun on her hunched shoulders. Loved to slide her kerchief off and feel the breeze in her hair. Loved to view the world from such a height. But not today. Today she had Leena Hakola.

"And the *lakka* berry," Leena continued. "Remember the *lakka*? There's nothing like the *lakka* in this country. I've never seen it. Have you? I don't suppose they grow here at all. Maybe in Minnesota. What do you think? Do you think the *lakka* grows in Minnesota? There are many Finns in Minnesota. And plenty of work on the iron range. Maybe the *lakka* grows there, too. What do you think? Do you think the *lakka* grows there?"

"No! It doesn't grow there at all!"

"Oh— But you remember the taste?"

Kaisa did remember the taste. She remembered it each June when the days were long and the summer heat was still a promise. Like a raspberry in shape but orange in color.

Low to the ground. A single berry to the stem. What Finn
didn't remember the *lakka* and long for its taste?

"Do you think I am so simple that I have lost my memory?
Of course I remember the *lakka*. You pick here," Kaisa said,
"and I'll go over there. That way we won't bother each
other."

Kaisa slid the pack that had grown heavy with the climb
from her shoulders and stood it against a rocky shelf that
glistened with strands of shining quartz. And then she
started to pick.

As the berries fell into the bucket, Kaisa' troubles with
Leena were forgotten. Her fingers worked quickly. The
round dusky-colored berries bounced, rolling in the empty
space, plopping softly as the bottom covered. Not a leaf, not
a stem, not a green berry marred the blue of the growing
mound. Her fingers flew. She breathed deeply and smiled,
pausing for an instant to look out over the world—the mountains, the woods, the farms, the village. God was with her.

She picked faster than ever. And the faster she picked, the
more she thought of Leena. And the more she thought of
Leena the more she realized how shamefully she had acted
towards her. But from this moment, she resolved, her heart
full of song, she'd be kinder. More understanding. Kaisa
clasped her hands together and bowed her head, her eyes
smarting. "Help me, Heavenly Father," she prayed. "Give
me patience and understanding. . . ."

Already the bucket was full. She carried it to the little
rock shelf where she had left the coffee. Reaching for the
still-warm jug, she filled one of the cracked mugs for herself,
and then, her heart glowing, she poured coffee into the
other mug as well and called, "Leena, come for coffee!"

"Coffee? Coffee? Just what I was waiting for," Leena
panted, even before Kaisa could screw the lid back onto the
coffee jug. "And, yes, I'll take a *korpu*, too." She crunched
one of the cinamon-and-sugar-sprinkled rusks, dribbling
crumbs down her narrow chin. "I've never made good
*korpu* myself," Leena said as she chewed the crusty bit.
"But I don't make good *nisu* either. And you need to make
good *nisu* to make good *korpu*, eh? Maybe you can show me,

eh? Then when Nestori gets back, I'll make good *korpu* so that he can take it in the woods for coffee. Ohhh—!'' she exclaimed, spying the bucket, mounded with firm plump berries. "You're full already? Look at my pail," she laughed, tilting the half-full lard pail for Kaisa to see. "Not as many. And not as clean as yours, eh?''

"Maybe if you'd save the eating for later, you'd have more!'' Kaisa snapped. Leena's mouth was stained dark with blue. And who'll clean those? Kaisa wondered. Leena's pail was messy with twigs and leaves. Her berries mushy. Not like Kaisa's, so clean and dry they wouldn't need to be picked over at all. But Leena's berries! Like Leena herself. Kaisa gulped her coffee and hurried off to fill the cooking pot.

As she picked, she heard a barking from below. Karhu? Was he chasing that bull? She should have known better than to leave him. Through the years they had had enough trouble with George Pottle, what with that cow they used to have getting into his corn. She stood, running her hand over the small of her back. Stiff. But the pot was filling. Just a while longer. Then home. But what about Leena? Probably still didn't have that first lard pail full. And messy! Never had Kaisa seen such messy berries.

Again she heard the faint barking from below.

At last she called out to Leena, "I'm going home. No. You stay," she said when Leena's unkempt head popped over the crest of the ridge. "My kettle is full. Matti will want to eat. You come for dinner when you're through.''

"But— '' Leena started.

"No. You stay and have a good time," Kaisa chirped. "So many nice berries. And I'll leave the rest of the coffee for you. By this rock. Do you see?'' she asked, holding up the woolen stocking, swollen with the jug inside.

Balancing the brimming cooking pot in the crook of one arm and the overflowing milk bucket in the other hand, Kaisa hurried off into the shadowy woods. With each step down the steep trail, she skirted twisted branches and loose rocks that threatened to send her flying. With each step, berries bounced from the too-full vessels. She tried holding the cooking pot by the handle but felt so unbalanced that the

walking was even more difficult. At last, though, her feet
found a rhythm.

*Well, Kaisa,* she found herself thinking, *you didn't keep
your resolve, did you? You're not acting very Christian
towards Leena.*

She snorted.

*You bully her.*

"I do not!" Kaisa's arms ached with the awkwardness
of carrying the berries.

*But she wanted to leave. She hates to pick berries. Any-
one can see that.*

At that moment, Kaisa stumbled, her foot catching on a
root that snaked from the ground. As she twisted to regain
her balance, berries bounced in the air. She straightened.
Although her heart was pounding, she felt smug that she
hadn't lost her grip on either the cooking pot or the milk
bucket. She blew at a wisp of hair that slid out from under
the kerchief and brushed against her nose. Her arms creaked
with stiffness.

Pausing to rest at the upper edge of the field, she stooped
to place first the milk bucket and then the cooking pot at her
feet. There was no sign of the dog. Nor could she see the
bull. To cross through the field would take but half the steps
of the rough trail. She looked to the sun. It was high. And
the bull was nowhere to be seen. Maybe sleeping under a
tree in the far corner. Or maybe Pottle had taken it in. She
remembered Leena back on the hilltop picking her messy
berries. She'd be coming along anytime. Talking. Talking.
Although it wasn't in her nature to be so, Kaisa's anger
towards Leena had made her reckless. Surely, she thought,
she was spry enough to cross that field in no time.

Kaisa reached over the stone wall and through the thick
strands of barbed wire to set the cooking pot and shiny milk
bucket on the other side. She found a spot where she could
crawl under the taut wire. As she inched through, her kerchief
caught and then the back of her skirt. "*Voi hyvänen aika!*"
she muttered, yanking at the kerchief until she heard a faint
tear. "Oh, for goodness sake!"

Picking up her berries, she stood to survey the field. It

was still enough. She wet her lips. Her mouth felt dry. She took one step. And then another.

The berries bounced as she walked, rolling to the ground. Nearly there, she thought, when the distance behind her equalled that yet to go. Her heart thumped against the metal of the cooking pot. She was walking quickly, one foot seemingly chasing the other.

She was almost running. The berries jounced into her path. She held her hand along the rim of the pot, trying to stop the flying berries. She saw where she would squeeze through the fence. Next to some young poplars.

She didn't hear but felt, through the soles of her hard black shoes, the thunder of the bull's approach. Her legs, entangled in the coarse dark material of her long skirt, groped mechanically. She clutched the cooking pot so that it dug into her arm. Still the round berries flew into the air. She knew she should drop them. She knew that the cooking pot and bucket impeded her flight but was unable to let them go. She turned and saw in a blinding instant the huge black bull bearing down on her.

She saw its head lower. The wide horns twist. Heat eased into the fleshy part of her, just below the ribs. Her neck spun and snapped. She knew not to move, to become as limp as the ragbag hanging in the woodshed, to not try again for the fence. Blueberries rained down on her, soft and cool. As gentle as spring mist.

Seconds or minutes or hours later, she lay with her face buried in sweet clover. She heard the far-off raspy call of a crow. From the great stillness, she knew that the bull was no longer there. Her head beat thickly. The berries? Where were the berries?

And then pain.

For a long while Kaisa lay still, her eyes too weighted to open. She knew that Matti would want his dinner, and she wondered whether he had thought to stir the beans. She groped for the knot in her kerchief, fumbling with it over the open wound. Her clothes were torn, the short jacket, her dark striped skirt.

Kaisa inched towards the fence. Leena. Leena would be

coming, would see. The prickly barbs of wire reached out, grabbed her.

She thought of the clock on the shelf between the two front windows. The steady tick. Never stopping. She looked to the glaring sun to judge the time. But she couldn't remember which way was east.

Matti would go for the doctor. She had never seen the doctor before. Had taken care of their ills herself. He would look at her, see such a private part. She wanted to get home to wash herself. The *sauna* would be cold. But there would be water. And soap.

Struggling to her feet, she glimpsed the faded purple kerchief, now darkly stained as she clutched it to herself. She fought back a rush of nausea. Again she remembered the *sauna*, needing to get there.

It was in the *sauna* that Leena found her.


For the better part of a week, Kaisa didn't know one day from another. She would wake and ask for water, seeing sometime Leena and sometime Matti. She fretted about the lost blueberries, begging Matti to go back and find them. Because he felt so helpless, Matti climbed to the ridge and filled the cooking pot and milk bucket he had earlier retrieved. The berries were as clean as though Kaisa herself had picked them. He carried them up to the loft bedroom to show his wife. She smiled and drifted off to sleep.

Perhaps it was the rooster's first tentative morning call, or perhaps it was the faint glow of dawn just painting the horizon that woke Kaisa. Or perhaps it was that she was hungry, hungrier it seemed than she could ever remember being. It was strange to her that she was alone in the room that she had shared with Matti all these years. She slid her feet onto the cool floor and tried to stand, but because of the nagging pull below her ribs and the weakness in her legs, she fell back onto the pillow.

She took assurance in the familiar shapes in the dusky shadows. The gentle curve of the footpiece of the iron bedstead. The cold bedroom stove with its long pipe. The smooth pitcher and bowl on the low commode. The gauzy curtain, barely stirring at the open window. From down below she heard Leena's voice, full of chatter so early in the morning. The dog Karhu barked from outside. The scent of coffee wafted upstairs, reminding her of her hunger.

She called to Matti, but her voice had no strength and wouldn't carry.

The sky turned from pink to violet, and although she had been watching, she wasn't able to say just when it happened.

She was instead remembering the fright. The heat. The pain. She remembered crawling through the fence, clutching the kerchief to her oozing hurt. She remembered the water spilling in *sauna*. Leena carrying her. Leena holding a cup for her to drink. Leena crooning as she changed the dressing.

Kaisa insisted that Matti help her down the stairs to the kitchen for breakfast. As Leena fluttered about, Kaisa sat at her place at the round table, a shawl over her shoulders, her long brown hair hanging loose.

"Soon you'll be as good as new," Leena clucked. "Oh my!" And she flittered to Kaisa's side, taking up her tired hand to kiss it. "Oh! You haven't eaten for five days. And now you're hungry, eh? I'll make you a good breakfast. Then you'll be strong. Five days!"

Although Kaisa lacked bodily strength, her sight was as good as ever. Already she had spotted yesterday's crumbs on the table. The bright runner that ran along the middle of the floor was stained; the other two gritty and askew. Dishes were piled at the sink.

She caught her husband's eye as she picked up a biscuit, the bottom as black as the stovetop. But she turned it to butter it, so the black wouldn't show. Leena hovered close by, tense as a bird ready for flight, while Kaisa took a spoonful of beans. Kaisa glanced at Matti who waited with a dribbling knifeful ready to shovel into his open mouth. Never had she tasted such salty beans! They were hot with salt.

"What beans!" she said, swallowing. "What beans! I now understand why Matti has talked about Leena's beans all these years." And then she added, "Leena, when I'm stronger, you should show me how to make these beans."

Pleasure flushed over Leena's face. "You like my beans, eh?" she asked, puffing with importance, hustling to the stove to scoop out more from the frying pan. "Now you go ahead and eat. Leena's beans will make you strong."

Kaisa nodded. She glanced at Matti and saw a smile twinkling in his eyes. "And while you're up, Leena, would you get me some water? The fever— It's made me so thirsty."

# THE WEDDING

1916

After *Komia* Nestori came for Leena Hakola, the house was strangely quiet. Kaisa Kilponen recovered from her misadventure with the bull more quickly than one would have expected and was soon up and about, but the days were long as she settled listlessly into her old routine. Even the brightness of autumn went with Leena, and already in early November, the earth was frozen and hollow-sounding underfoot.

Kaisa, clutching the thick collar of her heavy black coat, scuttled a step or two ahead of her husband. The fire in the church that Sunday morning had been started late, and its warmth never reached beyond the front pews. Kaisa was chilled through and through. Now she couldn't walk fast enough. All she could think about was getting home and building up the fires in her own kitchen and sitting room. Gravel crunched under her hard shoes. The sun was thin in a cold November sky.

A spindly red geranium on the front windowsill of the kitchen quivered. "Ooo— " Kaisa sighed as the heat from the cook stove at last penetrated the back of her plain dark skirt.

"It's already winter. And only November." At last the scent of strong coffee bubbling warmed her enough so that she could once again think about the good news.

Erkki and Mari Seilonen's oldest daughter Este was to be married to Lauri Marttinen, just six weeks from this very Sunday. And Lauri, being at least ten years older than Este and a steady, hard worker, had already put enough aside to buy a farm where he and his bride would set up housekeeping. What especially excited Kaisa was that this farm was on the very road on which she and Matti lived, just beyond George Pottle's. For years the house had stood empty. But now it would be the home of neighbors. Finnish neighbors.

"Imagine!" Kaisa said to her husband as she fanned the back of her skirt in front of the open oven door. "Este and Lauri. It will be like having relatives closeby." And after a long moment's thought, she added, "And don't you suppose that next year there might not be a little one? And when he's big enough, he'll come here to visit. I'll pour coffee for him. Just a little. With plenty of milk. And give him *nisu*. Or a cracker. Do you remember those two tiny cups Hilja Kyllonen gave me? I'll use those. And he'll think those cups are just for him. What do you suppose they'll name him?" Kaisa bustled to the pantry for two white mugs. "Erkki probably. Just like his grandfather."

"Woman! Lauri and Este aren't even married, and already you've named their first son!" Matti shouted, feigning annoyance so that the dog named Karhu, who drowsed in the corner, raised his head to look.

"Let's have a little something to eat and go to the Seilonen's this afternoon," Kaisa suggested. "We haven't been to visit for a long while. And then we can find out more about this wedding."

"On such a cold day?"

"It's not so cold."

"You complained all the way to church."

"That was earlier. It's much warmer now."

As reluctant as Matti was on that cold Sunday afternoon to leave the coziness of the house as well as the long nap he had been looking forward to, he succumbed to his wife's wheedling and harnessed one of the big brown horses to the express for the ride to the Seilonen's. The husband and wife sat beside each other on the high seat, a heavy buffalo robe wrapped over them.

The prospect of a wedding excited a romantic feeling in Kaisa that she, even as a young bride, had never indulged in. Times had been grim when she had arrived in America, uprooted from her homeland and thrust nearly penniless into a strange culture and even stranger language. Marriage had been a matter of necessity. For her, it had been one more aspect of the hard work of life.

But for Este, who had come to this country in her mother's arms, it was different. She had grown up in Edom. With her brothers, she had gone to one of the little schools that dotted the countryside. And Este could speak English, although she seldom did.

The other Seilonen offspring were visiting neighbors that afternoon, but Este was at home with her mother and father. It was she who made and served the coffee.

"What a good worker!" Kaisa exclaimed as Este came around the table to pour more coffee, first for the men and then for the women. Kaisa reached out and embraced Este around the hips, squeezing the folds of the voluminous white apron. "And so nicely rounded, too."

"And strong," Erkki said, pride glowing in his blue eyes. "She can pitch a load of hay as well as any man."

"Este's always been a big help," said Mari.

"Lauri is smart to take a Finnish wife. These American women don't know how to work. Not like a Finn," Matti remarked, his head bobbing.

Este, her back to the praise, stacked little sweet cakes onto a plate. A blush crept up the back of her neck and into the tight part that separated the two coils of white-blond hair.

"A good cook, too," Mari added, sliding the flowered plate of cakes closer to the men. "She's the one who made these. My Este! Never has she given me trouble. Not like the boys."

When the cakes were no more than a few last crumbs on the

plate, and the talk was turning to the price of pulpwood, Mari urged Kaisa into the parlor. The room was crowded with heavy dark furniture. Bric-a-brac overspread the two oval tables, covered with long fringed cloths. A small desk stood in the corner, its closed front decorated with a gracefully carved swirling filigree. Sober sepia-tinted photographs were mounted on the flowered walls. A warm fire crackled in the parlor stove, and pale afternoon light filtered through lace curtains.

"Your parlor is so comfortable. I could easily sit here all day. Now where's Este?" Kaisa said, stepping back into the shadowy little hallway. "Este," she called, "come now."

Kaisa settled back on one side of the stiff mounded cushion of the horsehair sofa. "Right here, Este," she insisted, patting the shiny seat beside her. "You come sit with me. I want to hear about your arrangements."

Este's round cheeks flushed as she perched next to Kaisa.

Edging closer, Kaisa demanded, "Well?"

"Go on, Este," Mari prompted from the low-backed oak rocker next to the heat of the parlor stove. "Tell Kaisa."

"Yes, tell me."

Este's white fingers flicked to her rosy cheek. Her eyes darted to her mother and then to the floor and back to her mother again. "We will . . . um . . . marry," she stammered. "And live near you. In that house." She exhaled, greatly interested in the flower and leaf design of the hooked rug at her feet.

"That's all?" Kaisa asked. "That's all?"

Este nodded, her eyes miserable.

Mari rocked, the caning in the chair creaking. *She* apparently saw nothing amiss in Este's plans.

"But this will be a big occasion!" Kaisa blurted. "So many people. Think about the food. What are you going to do about food?"

"Mother and I— "

"You and your mother have far too much to think about," Kaisa said in growing excitement. "You let me take care of the food. I'll see to everything. Tomorrow I'll go to Hilja Kyllonen's. She's sometimes lazy, but I'll tell her what to do.

And there are plenty of others who can work. They just need
to be told. There!" She leaned into the prickly horsehair.
"Tell me what you intend to wear. A wedding is an important
affair. What you wear could well influence the remainder
of your days."

"Mother and I— "

"Of course Este will have something new to wear," Mari
interrupted. "I plan to help her make a new skirt. We already
have some nice navy blue serge. And she has a piece of lace
that her godmother gave her on the day she was born. To
decorate the shirtwaist."

"Oh?" said Kaisa, sitting tall on the edge of the sofa.
"Oh? But this is America. In America women wear white
gowns when they marry. Don't you think that would be nice
for Este? Now, Mari—I should not have to tell you this—
Este is your oldest. You and Erkki have done well here.
Better than most. Este should have a white wedding gown.
Surely, you and I could make one. And you even have that
nice new Singer!" Kaisa waggled her stubby finger at Mari.
"Este, run and get the Sears-Roebuck catalog so we can see
what they have for material."

"But, Kaisa *täti*— " Este called Kaisa "aunt" as all the
Seilonen children did. "I— "

"I'll hear no words of protest!" Kaisa insisted, her eyes
closed. "It's the least that I can do. Now get the catalog."


In the waning glow of late afternoon, the horse plodded
along the hard gravel road. Kaisa smiled, snuggling into the
heavy buffalo wrapped over them.

After some time, Matti said, "Don't you think you're interfering a little too much?"

"Interfering? I'm not interfering!" Kaisa said in surprise.
"I'm helping."


It was the muffled quiet the morning after Lauri's and
Este's wedding that woke Kaisa. Snow was falling, and
already the earth was blanketed in white.

"What a good thing the wedding was yesterday and not today," Kaisa said, staring out the kitchen window, glazed with crystals of frost as delicate as the lace that had graced Este's white wedding dress. "Not many would have wanted to venture out on a day like this."

"Not many." Matti worked a patch onto the toe of a rubber boot.

"God was with them." Kaisa was recalling the feel of Mari Seilonen's hand in hers as they sat together on the women's side of the church. And as clearly as though it were occurring again in front of her, she saw Lauri and Este before the altar rail, just as they had stood the day before. "Do you think they're warm enough?" she suddenly asked.

"Who?"

"Este and Lauri! Do you think they're warm enough in that house?"

"They have plenty of firewood."

"But the wind is sure to come up. Their stoves might not draw."

"Lauri has lived there for over a month. Don't you think he could tell whether or not the stoves draw?"

All morning as Kaisa mixed and kneaded and baked bread, she fretted about Este and Lauri. Were they warm enough? Was Este lonely? Did they have enough food?

"Enough food?" Matti scoffed. "You were the one who put all the leftover food into Lauri's wagon. They have enough food for the whole winter, even if it doesn't melt until June." He went back to reading his week-old edition of *The County Observer*, rattling the pages and ignoring his wife, who cleared a small round spot on the frosty window with the tip of her finger to peer anxiously at the deepening snow.

Kaisa switched the flat bread pans from top to bottom and from bottom to top. Pushing the oven door closed, she said, "Este is used to having a big family about. That house must seem quiet to her now. Maybe she misses her mother."

Matti peered over the top of the newspaper. "You're not thinking of going there, are you?"

"Maybe they need something. Or they might want company."

"Company? They don't want company! Don't you remember, Kaisa, the day after *we* were married?"

At noon they had potato soup and bread. Matti repaired harness in the shed, and when his fingers grew numb with cold, he brought his work into the kitchen. Finally, that chore was through, and he stretched on the tufted bed couch in the sitting room, close to the crackling stove for an afternoon nap.

When he was comfortably sleeping, Kaisa wrapped two of the cooled loaves of crusty bread in a clean towel and tucked them snuggly into a knapsack made of woven birch. She pulled heavy stockings over her feet and fastened her sturdy boots. She shrugged the knapsack over the bulky material of her black coat, tied a woolen kerchief over her head and picked a pair of warm coarse mittens from the box behind the kitchen stove. She moved so stealthily through the kitchen that the only sound was the click of the outside door as she closed it. In the shed she found the narrow pointed skis that Matti had made many winters before and carried them out into the softly falling snow.

Silently, she pushed off with the long poles, gliding towards the snow-covered field rather than towards the road. The brushy coffee-colored dog Karhu barked twice and pranced beside her, stopping to roll in the fluffy white. Kaisa breathed the sharp cold air and glanced back over her shoulder as though to see whether or not Matti were watching. The trail she had left was straight. The house, her house, loomed through the soft puffy flakes. She hesitated and then started again, her skis swishing as she, in her long black coat and kerchief, crossed through the expanse of white towards the forest.

The woods were dark with fir and spruce and pine. Snow-covered branches drooped heavily over the tote road. Karhu, with his nose to the snow, scurried off into the brush, leaving a messy trail behind him. Kaisa clambered over a little stream, the water gurgling steel gray and cold against the pure white snow.

Her skis swooshed, a pleasant sound in the deep stillness. Not a squirrel, not a bird, not even the wind broke the silence. There was only the sound of her skis.

She left the tote road, gliding into a small ravine and then making her way uphill, over and through clumps of trees and fallen limbs and brush. At last she skied out of the woods, on the road beyond George Pottle's.

She blinked in the unexpected brightness, for the clouds had parted and a weak sun shone through the falling snow. Snowflakes, fat and wet, caught on the black wool of her coat. Tomorrow, she knew, would be cold. The wind was sure to howl around the corners of the house and sift through the window sashes and flail the new snow across open fields. But for today, the world was still, a gentle quiet land of clean white.

She skimmed over the fresh snow until she came to a small rise where she could look down on the weathered house and aged barn, the home now of Lauri and Este. Lauri had his work before him. The barn and house cried for repair. Fences were down. Fields were growing over. Their own farm had been no better. But Matti had worked hard, clearing hay fields and adding new land as he could.

Kaisa leaned on her poles, shrugging the pack on her back to balance it. She watched a wisp of smoke wafting from the chimney, the late afternoon sun glinting golden from the four windows to the west, the snow like a bed of down around the ramshackle buildings.

A chickadee sounded closeby, breaking into her thoughts, and flitted past to perch on a slender twig, bejeweled with small red berries. A last wet flake landed on her warm cheek and melted. The gray shingled house was snug and secret.

The corners of Kaisa's mouth rounded into a smile. And then, as quietly as she had come, she turned to glide back towards the deep stillness of the forest.

# TIN POURING

1918

"The men are into the cider," Kaisa Kilponen whispered to Elvi Laurila. The two women, their cheeks glowing pink from an earlier *sauna*, came from the sitting room where Hilja Kyllönen rocked Este Marttinen's whimpering baby boy.

"There's no stopping them when there's a cider barrel," Elvi said, her voice, as always, bubbling laughter. She trailed Kaisa into the pantry. "We can overlook it tonight. It's New Year's Eve."

"You know how Hilja— "

"Oh, never mind Hilja. She's so busy telling Este how to care for that baby— Here, let me help." She reached for the plate of cardamom-flavored buns.

"Perhaps the cider will loosen Matti. He says pouring tin is old-fashioned, a silly superstition from the old country, that we shouldn't be doing it here." Kaisa sliced a pound cake, rich with butter and fresh eggs.

"What's that?" Hilja Kyllönen's broad round face appeared over Elvi's shoulder.

"Matti thinks we shouldn't pour tin," Elvi quickly ex-

113

plained, catching Kaisa's eye. "He says it's a silly custom."

"We always do it for the New Year! What harm is there in keeping an old custom?" Hilja's upper lip, lately grown fuzzy, quivered. "Where are the men? I know I heard them come in from *sauna*."

"There they are!" said Kaisa, cocking her head at the familiar creak to the cellar stairs. "Here, Hilja, you can put the rice pies on the table. Elvi, you can take the cream."

Kaisa poured coffee, first for the men and then for the women. "The table is sparse tonight, but— "

"We all have to ration," said Elvi.

"You have more than we need," Este added. "And what you make is always delicious."

"No, no," Kaisa denied, although she did flush with pleasure. "It's plain food. Nothing much. Elvi, when you go home, take something for your boys. I wish they had come, but if Janne isn't well, I suppose it's not good to go out in the cold."

"It's too cold for anyone to be out," said Hilja.

"This weather would feel warm if we were in Finland," Tuomo said, buttering a slice of rice pie. "We've been here so long, we've almost forgotten how cold it got back there."

"How did we say it? When you take a leak, it freezes before it hits the ground." A smile twitched at the corners of Matti's mouth.

With color seeping along the tight part that separated the white-blond braids wound over her head, Este smirked into her hand.

As they ate, they laughed and talked about old times, occurrences in Finland and in America. Then the talk drifted, as most talk did of late, to their homeland's efforts to declare itself free of Russian rule.

"They could wake up at any time and reclaim Finland," Tuomo said thoughtfully, scratching a match over his thumbnail to light a freshly rolled cigarette."

"They have too much to think about now with their own

revolution to care about Finland." Matti spoke with force. This was not the first time he had uttered these same words, but in their repetition, they seemed to ring more heavily with truth. The good humor of the evening ebbed as he was once again beset with the uneasiness that had haunted him.

"They'll need access to the Baltic," Lauri added. Although slight and by nature reserved, when Lauri spoke, he spoke with authority.

"The bear will be scratching at the door," said Tuomo, inhaling deeply so that his nostrils quivered. "Mark my words."

"If you ask me," Hilja blurted, "Finland should not upset the cart. It can only go worse later on when Russia realizes what it has lost."

"You're saying that we should be happy to be a part of Russia? Of no more significance than a small toe?" Anger showed in Matti's face. "That stupid talk is nothing but woman's talk!"

"Matti!" Kaisa's cup clattered onto the rose-rimmed saucer. "Hilja is our guest."

"How can you think like that?" Matti continued, ignoring his wife. "Finland is in the midst of its greatest struggle— "

"That may be true," Elvi added, her voice shaking, "but we hear so little. We have relatives. We have no idea what— "

"We are all concerned!" Hilja snapped, her back stiff. "There's no call to— "

"Have you so quickly forgotten those years of famine and suppression?" Matti spoke louder. "Have you forgotten? Or had you already gone?"

"There's not a one of us who will ever forget. Speak for yourself. Haven't you become an American citizen?"

Matti's eyes flashed. Hilja's words smacked against the root of his uneasiness. Guilt at having left his people behind. Shame at not being there in Finland's time of trouble.

A weighty silence hung over the warm kitchen. Lauri gulped his coffee. Hilja moved her chair. Este coughed.

From the bed couch in the sitting room, the baby cried out so that Este leapt from the table, upsetting the nearly full cup before her. Milky coffee seeped into the linen cloth and drizzled to the floor.

"Never mind!" Kaisa insisted, scurrying for a cloth, as Este fluttered, trying to stop the dripping coffee. At last, she rushed into the sitting room to tend her child.

"Well," Kaisa exclaimed, once the coffee had been sopped from the table and floor. "It's New Year's Eve. The tin is ready. Shall we look into the future?"

"Here we are in America, the most modern country in the world," Matti muttered. "Gas lights. Telephones. Automobiles. And still you women pour tin."

"No harm," Tuomo laughed. "Let them do it. We might learn something."

Matti scoffed.

"Back in Finland," Hilja said, bobbing her head so that her cheeks wobbled, "we poured tin the year we came to this country. It was all there, the prophecy that we would come."

"You knew you were coming!"

"No, it was the tin."

"We always poured tin in my uncle's family," Lauri said. "Then when he died, we stopped doing it."

"It's just a custom," Elvi added, her eyes smiling. "We do it for fun."

"Never mind him," Kaisa said to the women as they cleared the table. "He thinks we should forget all the old customs."

"It will be the *sauna* next!" Tuomo said, slapping Matti on the shoulder. "Then you can take a bath in a wash tub like the Yankees."

Matti snatched the lantern from the shelf and rushed for the door to the cellar stairs.

When Matti returned, carrying three brimming mugs of cider, Hilja was shaking the long-handled dipper over the heat of the stove. She glanced up as Matti handed a full mug to each of the other men. "Cider? Didn't you make a pledge? Just last month?"

Twisting her fingers, Elvi interrupted brightly, "We've just learned that Lauri and Este are going to have a large family. Eight children! Isn't that so, Este?"

Este blushed. "That's what was in the tin," she said.

"My advice is not to save the daughters for last," said Elvi. "You're going to need help with all that washing."

"Horse manure!" Matti sidled to the table, slouching into one of the straight-backed chairs.

Ignoring Matti, Hilja asked, "Who wants to pour now? Elvi? Tuomo?"

"Tuomo can pour. I don't like to." Elvi nudged her husband closer to the stove. "Tuomo, you do it."

With the quilted holder, Tuomo grasped the handle. As the stream of melted tin struck the cold water, it cracked and sizzled. "It looks like a boat. A tar boat."

"No, I'd say a church boat." Hilja took the wet tin shape from Tuomo's hand. "It's too deep for a tar boat."

"But there are no church boats here in America," Este protested.

"It doesn't mean that there has to be a church boat here. It's what it represents that is important. It must be a journey of some sort. Most likely a sacred journey."

Kaisa's eyes danced. "Maybe you'll return to Finland! After the war, of course. Oh, Elvi! And on Sundays you'll take the boat to church just like we used to."

"It's probably that *other* journey," Matti sneered, tapping his mug against the edge of the table. "You know the one I mean. The *last* one."

Hilja frowned but said, "Did I ever tell you about the time the church boat overturned?"

Kaisa shook her head.

"When I was a girl," Hilja began, "my mother and our neighbor Mimmi Koskela had a falling out. Mimmi made an image of Mother from rags and some straw and then tied a knot in one of the legs so that my mother suffered terrible pain."

"Like you!" Kaisa interjected. "You, too, have that same pain. Maybe that was the cause of your pain as well."

"Kaisa, this happened years ago. Now, let me finish." As she continued, she placed the lump of tin into the dipper, returning it to the stove. "It was Easter. Since that spring happened to be unusually mild, and the ice was out early, we were able to take the church boats for Easter services.

Somehow one of the boats overturned. Can you imagine how
it was? The water so cold at that time of year. But except
for one, all were saved.''

"Was that Mimmi?" Elvi asked, her arms crossed snugly
over her bosom as she listened.

"It was. Mimmi Koskela. That's not the end of it, though.
Afterwards, a young boy said that he had seen what looked
to be a hand reaching out from the lake for her.

"Some said it was the hand of the devil seeking his own.
Now, I don't know about that. What I do know is that the boy
was pious enough. At age ten, he had read the Bible from
cover to cover. Try as they did, her body was never found.''

"The hand of the devil," Matti mimicked, sitting apart.
"The old enemy. Satan himself."

"I'm just telling you what they said. Who am I to dispute
them? But as for you, Tuomo and Elvi, there will be a journey.
A journey as sacred as that of a church boat on Easter Sunday."

Elvi smiled at Tuomo, her pale eyes wide.

"Kaisa, the tin is ready." Hilja held the holder out.

"No. You do it first. You're the guest."

"Go ahead, Hilja," Elvi urged. "Maybe you'll find yourself on that journey with us."

"Such an old woman? No, my traveling days are over."
She gripped the handle and poured. Again, the hot tin cracked
against the water.

Hilja plucked the drippng shape, an uneven rectangular
figure.

"It's a coffin," Elvi whispered.

Matti jumped from the table to snatch the tin from Hilja's
hand. "It doesn't look like a coffin to me! It's only a mess of
tin. How can you call this a coffin? Are you going to freeze
to death on the way home? Or will the horse trample you?"
He squeezed the uneven shape with such force that it buckled.
"Is that what you think?"

Este edged closer to her husband. "We should take Juha
home. It's late."

"Wrap him well. It's cold. I'll get the horse." He shrugged
into his thick woolen coat and cap as he spoke.

"And we, too, should go," Elvi said. "Hilja, get your things."

When the bells on the horses' harnesses were no more than hollow echoes, Kaisa finally said to Matti, "What about you? Are you going to bed?"

He slouched at the table, picking splintered edges from the ragged piece of tin. "I think I'll stay up for a while. I'm not sleepy."

"Keep away from that cider! You've had enough for one night. Already you've forgotten your pledge. And insulting our company like that. You know how Hilja will talk."

Although the Finnish language newspaper was spread before him, Matti did not read. Instead, he thought about Finland, the family and friends he had left behind. He had been only a boy, although he had thought himself a man, fired with a passion for adventure and new sights.

From outside, he heard the wind. The dog Karhu whined to be let inside. The clock between the two frosted windows ticked its steady rhythm.

Matti opened the door for the coffee-colored dog, now white around its muzzle. He added more wood to the fires, both in the kitchen and sitting room, and again went down to the cellar for a last mug of cider.

Back at the table, Matti thought about Finland's shaky avowal of independence and the struggle that was sure to beset his people. As he drank, he toyed with the piece of tin and then shoved it aside. As though tin could be a prediction of things to come!

The dog sighed from behind the stove. The clock struck eleven, momentarily filling the warm room with sound. Afterwards, there was only the steady tick. Matti yawned.

Karhu whimpered in his sleep. It was then that Matti saw he wasn't alone.

Across the table sat a stranger, broad of shoulder and muscular of build, yet oddly frail as well. He had the plain, solid look of any Finn—pale, thin hair, a high forehead, and colorless eyes. His blouse of homespun was soiled and stained.

"Who are you?" Matti demanded. "Why are you here?" He knew, somehow, that this stranger had come from afar. "You must be tired and thirsty," Matti said. "I'll get you some cider. It's good. You'll like it."

In no time, Matti was back from the cellar, carrying two dripping mugs of cold cider. "Drink up," he urged, downing his own.

It surprised him to see that the stranger's mug was now empty, although he couldn't recall having seen him drink. Matti leaned towards him. "So tell me, how does it go there? Is there fighting?" He closed his eyes, for the room seemed to whirl. "How can such a poor country survive?"

Matti held the long-handled dipper. The tin had dissolved into a shimmering pool. The visitor stood behind him, close enough that his breath was warm.

A silvery stream leapt from the dipper in Matti's hand to explode in the bucket of water.

"Heh! Heh!" Matti sniggered. "I didn't— Didn't think it would be so loud. Sh— Sh— " He put a warning finger to his lips. His head wanted to roll forward. "Kai-sa. Don't wake Kai-sa."

He took the wet tin from the bucket. "What is it?" he asked, although he could plainly see.

In his hand was a rearing lion. On its bristled head was a crown, and it clutched in its forepaw a double-edged sword. Its tongue flickered, a fiery flame.

It seemed that it moved in his hand.

"But what does it mean?" he said.

Again, he felt it quiver.


Neither Matti nor Kaisa spoke the next morning as they sat for breakfast of porridge and rye bread. The only sound was the chinking of Kaisa's spoon against the side of her dish.

"Perhaps it will snow," she said, at last breaking the silence. "It's cloudy." With her teeth, she tore off a piece of chewy crust. "Did you pour tin last night?"

"Pour tin? You know I don't— "

Jabbing her finger at the odd tin shape next to the bowl of sugar spoons, she asked, "Well, what is that? Too much cider. That's your problem."

Matti snatched up the nubbly form.

"And all that noise. Who were you talking to?"

Matti looked around the simple kitchen—the stove, the curtained windows to the front, the clock, the corner cupboard, the bright floor runners. "I wasn't talking to anyone."

"I didn't think I would ever get to sleep. You were so noisy."

Matti rubbed the top of his head, the hair so thin that he was nearly bald. "I let the dog in— " he said aimlessly. He remembered the silent stranger, the roar of the fire, the feel of the lion, solid in his hand. It had been a prophecy. Of that, he had no doubt. He looked at the calendar above the woodbox. It was the first day of the new year, 1919.

"I told you to stay away from that cider." Kaisa stacked the plates together and stood to brush the crumbs from the table into her hand.

Matti arched his shoulders and stretched. He started to laugh, a laugh that grew from the very center of himself. As Kaisa bent to clean the table in front of him, he slapped her on the rump. *"Onelista Uttavuota!"* he shouted. "Happy New Year!"

# BOOKS BY PUCKERBRUSH PRESS

| | | |
|---|---|---|
| THE THOUSAND SPRINGS | short stories | Mary Gray Hughes |
| THE INVADERS | short storeis | Marjorie Kaplan |
| DRIFTWOOD | Maine stories | Edward Holmes |
| CIMMERIAN | poems | Constance Hunting |
| AN OLD PUB NEAR THE ANGEL | short stories | James Kelman |
| DORANDO: A SPANISH TALE | novel | James Boswell edited by Robert Hunting |
| THE CROSSING | poems | Albert Stainton Rita Stainton |
| THE MOUNTAIN, THE STONE | short stories | Kathleen Kranidas |
| A DAY'S WORK | poems | Michael McMahon |
| A PAPER RAINCOAT | poems | Sonya Dorman |
| BEYOND THE SUMMERHOUSE | poem | Constance Hunting |
| A STRANGER HERE, MYSELF | short stories | Thelma Nason |
| farmwife | poem | lee sharkey |
| GREENGROUND-TOWN | short stories | Christopher Fahy |
| BETWEEN SUNDAYS | short narratives | Douglas Young |
| ONE TO THE MANY | poems | Anne Hazlewood-Brady |
| NOTES FROM SICK ROOMS | essay | Mrs. Leslie Stephen |
| TWO PLAYS | plays | Arnold Colbath |
| WRITINGS ON WRITING | essays | May Sarton |
| box of roses | poems | lee sharkey |
| DEAD OF WINTER | poems | Michael McMahon |
| DARKWOOD | poems | Michael Alpert |
| THE POLICE KNOW EVERYTHING | Downeast stories | Sanford Phippen |
| THE ROCKING HORSE | sermons for children | Douglas Young |
| IN A DARK TIME | anthology | Virgil Bisset and Constance Hunting, editors |
| LIGHT YEARS | poems | Roberta Chester |
| MY LIFE AS A MAINE-IAC | autobiography/history | Muriel Young |
| PALACE OF EARTH | poems | Sonya Dorman |
| DEAREST ANDREW | letters | V. Sackville-West edited by Nancy MacKnight |
| THE DEATH OF MICHELANGELO | sonnet sequence | Jonathan Aldrich |
| A PRIMER OF CHRISTIANITY AND ETHICS | essays | Douglas Young |
| LETTERS TO MAY | letters | Eleanor Mabel Sarton |
| TURNIP PIE | short stories | Rebecca Cummings |